Micheala Lynn

AT ALL
COSTS

2016

Bella Books, Inc.
P.O. Box 10543
Tallahassee, FL 32302

Printed in the United States of America on acid-free paper.

First Bella Books Edition 2016

Editor: Cath Walker
Cover Designer: Sandy Knowles

ISBN: 978-1-59493-522-0

Other Bella Books by Micheala Lynn

Jagged Little Scar
Joie de Vivre

Acknowledgments

Special thanks to Esther Baugher for her painstaking help with all my medical questions. Any errors are on me and not her assistance or nursing expertise.

Again, thanks to Cath Walker, editor extraordinaire. As always, her advice and patience helped to bring this novel alive.

About the Author

Micheala Lynn divides her passions between writing, playing a wide variety of music, mountain biking, snuggling with her partner of many years on cold Michigan nights and home schooling their daughter. When not at her desk, she can be spotted on the local mountain biking trails or at a Renaissance Faire speaking Old English and playing the Scottish smallpipes. Her degrees include English Literature and Language, Anthropology and a Master's in Creative Writing, all from Central Michigan University. Find out more at www. MichealaLynn.com.

Dedication

To anyone who has refused to hear the word limitations and has pushed on at all costs. Never lose sight of the next finish line.

PROLOGUE

Jess's thoughts were lost in the rhythmic pounding of her feet on the pavement. After a long day, there was no better feeling than a late evening run. The cool, late October breeze provided a welcome chill to the heat boiling off her skin. But it was the heat deep down, further in where no cool breeze could touch, that was now occupying her mind.

She pulled up at the intersection, jogging in place and waiting for the light to change, her fingers to her neck checking her pulse—safely in the one thirties, but no surprise there. But how much of that was due to running or the memory of last night? A wide, lazy smile curled her lips. Oh, what a night it had been. Even now, almost twenty-four hours later, and she could feel her body responding once again. If she closed her eyes, she could picture every kiss, every caress, every hot, passionate moment. She had touched and been touched in ways she had never realized were possible, and with a woman. It felt wonderful, natural, right. Any doubt had completely gone.

She was gay, no denying it any longer.

The light changed and she took off again, lengthening her stride, with each reverberating step feeling the muscles still tender from last night's intimate activities. One, two, three, four—she counted off the steps as her feet hit the pavement. A part of her, a bigger part than she would have thought, wished that she could have spent the night with Tracy again. Just the thought of her name—Tracy—sent a fresh shudder through her body. But she needed some time, they both did, to come to terms with everything.

She had to laugh. Come to what terms? From the moment she had met Tracy, she knew that she would be the one—the one that would knock down those carefully constructed walls she had lived with for so long. Of course, she had wondered. She had always been different. She had never been interested in men, but to be gay? Could she accept that? And what about her family and friends? The only thing she knew for sure was that she wanted to be with Tracy in every way possible. Everything else would have to work itself out.

With all that whirling around in her head, she continued to push herself along, her heart thundering and beads of sweat trickling down her face. The sun was beginning to set, just tipping the tops of the trees in a golden orange glow. She closed her eyes, breathing in the wonderful autumn air, feeling it sear her throat and lungs with each breath. Suddenly, the screeching howl of tires on pavement broke the stillness. Jess whipped around quickly to catch a glimpse of the truck sliding right at her. As if in slow motion, she opened her mouth, forming a perfect O, and then—

CHAPTER ONE

Ten years later

Dr. Alexandra Hartway ran down the sidewalk, cursing under her breath. She glanced at her watch again. "Dammit." She was late—very late. If there was one thing she hated the most, it was being late. But this wasn't her fault. Today it seemed as if every freak, wacko and garden-variety nut job had decided to visit her ER. Then five minutes before her shift was to end, a middle-aged woman who looked at least twenty years older than her actual age rolled in claiming so much pain she couldn't walk. A quick look at her history showed this wasn't her first go—it wasn't even her tenth. Twelve trips over the past thirty-six months, all seeking the same thing.

The woman was a narcotic hound. After being told she wasn't getting a script, Ms. Can't-Walk-I'm-in-so-Much-Pain went into fifteen minutes of hysterics and threats. Not until security arrived did the woman leap from the wheelchair and dash out the doors as if someone had fired a starter pistol. Hallelujah, and the lame shall walk. And it wouldn't have been that big a deal if it hadn't been the fifth person *that shift* seeking narcotics. On

top of it all, Alex had been on call the previous night and ended up pulling a double shift. She wasn't as young as she used to be. Oh, the joys of being an ER doc.

She glanced down at her watch again. Great. She was beyond late, venturing into the land of no-show, and she still had a good three blocks to go. Everyone was going to think she was a flake being that this was her first time attending a board of directors meeting for the newly-formed Lesbian Professionals of West Michigan. Why had she let Jamie and her partner Sue, her two best friends, talk her into this anyway? They were always doing things like that—the fundraiser and gala for the Humane Society, March on the Capital for Equality, Ride for a Cure— she couldn't count the number of things Jamie had involved her in. For the most part, she couldn't complain.

But after her day in the ER, her heart really wasn't in it. If she hadn't promised, she'd be on her way home to soak in a warm bath, a full glass of wine in one hand, a heaping bowl of ice cream in the other, and listening to an audiobook until her skin wrinkled to the point that would make a prune jealous.

She finally rounded the corner, only half a block to go. They were meeting at The Station, a trendy new bar that opened a month ago in the renovated former Pearl Street fire station. As she scurried up to the front steps, she noticed a young man in his early thirties climb out of a new Dodge Charger parked in a handicap spot, handicap permit hanging from the rearview mirror, and jog across the street. When he reached the sidewalk, he continued jogging, weaving in and out of the foot traffic with all the ease of a NFL running back. Alex clenched her teeth. Figures. Here she had to walk how many blocks because she couldn't find a parking spot and this jackass parked right out front with a handicap permit he obviously didn't need. When had people become so lazy?

Still irascible, she stomped up the steps and through the front door. The bar was a cavern, dark and atmospheric, like a speakeasy from the thirties. Soft jazz played from the overhead speakers. Alex pondered what vice might have lurked in its dimly lit corners. Not difficult to imagine Don Corleone sitting

back there with his acolytes, obscured in smoke, discussing the family business.

As Alex peered through the gloom, she spied Jamie waving her over to her table. It looked like there might be half a dozen other women there, including Sue.

"Hey you made it." Jamie jumped up as she approached and gave her a hearty hug. Her dark blue, tailored, pinstripe suit perfectly complemented her golden blond, short-cropped hair. Jamie was the picture of a young professional businesswoman, a far cry from Alex's dull blue scrubs. If only she had had time to change.

"Finally." Alex rolled her eyes as she wrapped her arms around Jamie.

Sue pushed out the chair beside her. "We were beginning to wonder if you'd make it." Like Jamie, Sue was dressed impeccably in a long-sleeved white silk blouse and crisply-pressed tan slacks. Her hair was short and styled identically to Jamie's, the only difference being Sue's raven-black tresses versus Jamie's blond.

"Sorry I'm late. I got hung up at work." Alex felt like a ragamuffin compared to the other elegant women around the table.

Jamie clapped her on the back. "Don't worry about it. We were just chatting over drinks anyway." She quickly waved their waitress over.

Alex wasted no time ordering a red wine and as it arrived, Jamie lifted her glass. "Now that we're all here, I'd like to introduce Alex Hartway, perhaps the world's best ER doc and my best friend."

"I wouldn't say *best*." Alex could feel her cheeks beginning to flush. Leave it to Jamie. Her flair for the dramatic never failed to embarrass her.

"Whatever, you're the best ER doc *I* know."

Alex shook her head. What Jamie always neglected to add was she was the *only* ER doc, or any doctor for that matter, that Jamie knew.

Completely unperturbed, Jamie continued. "Now going around the table—" she indicated the woman sitting on Sue's other side, a tall, curly-haired brunette in a tweed blazer "—this is Ann Hutchinson. She is the director of the Milton E. Ford LGBT Resource Center at Grand Valley State."

Ann raised her glass. "Glad to meet you."

"Next, in the long white dreads, we have Terra Veenstra. Her family owns Infinity Books where she's the promotions manager."

Alex tried not to stare but she could safely say that she had never met anyone with more tattoos on her upper chest and arms than Terra, and where any given night in the ER could be a freak show, that was saying a lot.

"Beside her, we have another newbie—Jess Bolderson. Jess also works with Terra at Infinity Books and runs the printing thingy or whatever it's called."

"The Espresso Book Machine?" Jess leaned forward out of the shadows, her head cocked to the side.

Alex sucked in a quick breath. With her mind on her crazy day and being late, she hadn't really looked at everyone around the table. Still, how could she have missed the woman sitting directly across from her? With her small heart-shaped face, dark brunette pixie hair and deep brown eyes, she looked as if she could be a runway model or a stand-in for Emma Watson after she had cut off her Hermione curls.

Whoever the next two were at the table, Alex never heard. Jamie's voice was garbled background noise. She couldn't pull her eyes from the woman sitting across from her who was now chatting with long white dreadlocks. Finally a hefty jab in the ribs by Sue's elbow broke the trance.

"Sorry. *What?*" Again, she could feel her cheeks flushing. Talk about getting caught with the proverbial hand in the proverbial cookie jar.

Sue laughed. "I was just asking what held you up at work? I thought you said you'd be here a half hour ago."

"You know me, there's always something coming up." At least Sue hadn't noticed her fixation. If she had, Sue would tease her

for the next month. Then again, she probably deserved it. How many dates had she been on in the last year—two, maybe three? She wasn't exactly a major player when it came to romance. Didn't help that she carefully guarded what precious free time she had. With her job, she definitely needed some me time to wind down and recharge. Call it selfish, call it self-centered, call it what you will, but she didn't like to give up *her* time for anyone. Anyone except for Jamie and Sue—she could never say no to them. She took a long drink. "But I'll tell you what, you wouldn't believe the day I've been having."

Jamie joined in. "Why, what's going on?"

She took another long sip, nearly emptying it, and launched into the incident at the hospital. She knew enough about the laws and HIPAA privacy rules not to give away any personal details, but she could certainly share the gist of the situation. "...oh, she was in so much pain she couldn't walk." She rolled her eyes.

By now, everyone around the table was listening but no one quite as intently as Jess. She sat directly across, her eyes seemingly unblinking.

"Just another drug seeker, see it all the time." Alex drained her glass. "When I refused to give her a script, she started ranting and creating an almighty ruckus as if that would somehow change my mind. But get this, the moment security arrived, she literally sprints out." She motioned to their waitress for a refill.

Jess leaned forward. "What if she really did need help and all you did was threaten her?"

Alex tipped up her fresh glass of wine. "Oh please. The only thing she needed was perhaps a stint in rehab."

"Maybe that's why so many handicapped people are so leery of going to the hospital. They're afraid they'll be treated as druggies or liars." There was a definite edge to Jess's voice now.

"It's not like that. We see a lot of people with legitimate problems, handicapped and not. It's the ones that use a handicap as an excuse that get me."

By now, the rest of the table was watching the verbal tennis match.

"So, what you're saying is being handicapped is an excuse."

"That's not it at all. What I'm saying is some people use it as an excuse for laziness."

Jess flung up her hand clad in a black leather fingerless cycle glove and jabbed a finger at her. "Oh, so now you're saying some handicapped people are lazy." Sarcasm dripped from every word.

Alex let out an exasperated sigh. What the hell had she done to piss the girl off? All she'd been doing was sharing a story from work for why she was late. "You must admit, that happens often enough. For example, I had to park five blocks away but when I got here some guy parked right out front in a handicap spot with a permit hanging from his rearview only to jump out and go jogging up the street. If that's not laziness, I don't know what is."

From beside Jess, Terra was quickly waving her hand across her throat, her white dreadlocks flying. Sue nudged her with a toe under the table. Jamie placed her hand on Alex's arm and gave her a pointed look. "Alex."

Alex took a deep breath. This conversation had turned into a disaster. So much for kicking back and relaxing. She was tired, and more sensitive than she really should be. She should probably just chalk it up to a bad day and head on home.

Jess was still staring daggers at her, her nostrils flaring with each breath. "The handicapped people that *I* know are *anything* but lazy. Every day they work hard to overcome unbelievable obstacles, ongoing medical conditions, ease of access, ignorant people, simple things that regular people take for granted. It's no picnic, I can assure you."

Alex rubbed her forehead. She was really regretting opening her mouth. Talk about making a great first impression. This was supposed to be a meeting to promote a group for lesbian professionals and somehow it had turned into a catastrophe of a discussion about the disabled. "Look, I didn't mean to come across like that. Sometimes I wish that more people would work harder to help themselves. I mean I absolutely understand how lucky I've been. I've been blessed with good health. I have the

resources to maintain a healthy lifestyle. I still have to exercise, I run fifteen miles a week religiously, I eat right, I work hard to maintain a proper weight. I understand that not everyone can do that and look after their health."

"Yes, I agree. Everyone should be responsible when it comes to their health." Jess was calming down. At least she was no longer looking as if she were about to haul off and throw her drink across the table at her anymore.

Alex relaxed. The tension from the conversation seemed to be diffusing. "Exactly. I mean, just look at you. You're obviously health-conscious and in good shape. You look like you work out regularly..." That was an understatement. She couldn't help but admire Jess's long, lean muscular arms and well-built shoulders. From the looks of it, the girl had to be a bodybuilder or something. "...with a body like that you certainly can't complain."

"Alex!" Sue hauled off and kicked her under the table.

Pain shot up her leg and Alex rounded on Sue. "Ouch! What was that for?"

Sue quickly jerked her head toward the other side of the table.

Alex turned just in time to see Jess grab the table with her leather-clad hands and shove back. At first, she felt as if her mind had suddenly shifted into neutral. The whole scene took place in slow motion. Jess rolled a good three feet before she grabbed the wheels of her chair, coming to an abrupt halt. "Really? Can't complain?" Her face was beet-red and she seemed to be searching for more to say but finally just shook her head and, with a fierce thrust of her hands against her wheels, sent her chair flying across the restaurant.

The entire table let out a collective gasp. Sue kicked Alex in the leg again. Jamie shouted, "Alex!" Terra stood up, her dreadlocks flying, shot her a filthy look, threw a twenty-dollar bill down on the table and stormed out. Everyone else at the table turned and stared at her.

Feeling as if time had slowed to a crawl, Alex followed Jess's departure with her eyes glued to her back, trying her best to

wrap her mind around what had just happened. A wheelchair. The girl was in a wheelchair. How had she not noticed that? The leather gloves, the strong muscular shoulders, the chair. She hadn't been that big an idiot, had she? To no one in particular, she mumbled, "Why didn't someone tell me she's in a wheelchair?"

"Duh." Sue looked at her completely nonplussed. "Why do you think I kept kicking you under the table?"

Alex closed her eyes, held her hand up against her head and grimaced. "*That* was why she was so sensitive to what I said."

"You think?" Jamie stared wide-eyed. "Jesus, Alex, couldn't you see she was in a wheelchair?"

"I had no idea. When I first got here my eyes hadn't adjusted yet and she was on the other side of the table. I couldn't tell. It just looked like any other chair until she pushed back from the table." Even as Alex tried to rationalize what she had said, it felt weak to her ears. She couldn't ever remember feeling like a bigger ass. And rightly so. Talk about putting her foot in her mouth. If the sour taste in the back of her throat were any indication, that foot was also wearing the nastiest shoe imaginable.

* * *

"Hey Jess, wait up." Terra burst through the doors of The Station and hustled down the sidewalk.

Jess grabbed her wheels, feeling the heat from the friction against her gloves, and came to an abrupt halt. She wheeled around so fast she nearly knocked Terra off her feet.

Terra was gasping for breath. "Are you all right?"

That was all the opening she needed. Everything that she had wanted to say, that she should have said, came pouring out. "What a bitch! Who the hell does she think she is? Can you believe what she was saying? Lazy? *Lazy?* Who the hell is she to judge, all high and mighty?"

Terra took a step back from the force of her words. "Yeah, you've got that right—what a bitch. I couldn't believe she was saying that stuff. And she's a *doctor*."

Jess snorted and rolled her eyes. "Doctor, my ass. Jack the Ripper himself would make a better doctor than her. Remind me to never go to her hospital. I'd be better off with leeches and bloodletting."

Terra burst out laughing. "I don't doubt it. I can't believe she's a friend of Sue and Jamie's. They're always so sweet. But that Alex, she's just...just..."

"A bitch!"

"Yeah, a bitch." Terra held her hands up in mock defeat. "I guess there's no other way to describe her. I'm just sorry you had to go through that, this being your first time. I swear, it's never like that."

Jess waved her off. "Don't worry about it, Ter. It's nothing I haven't encountered before."

"Still." Terra let out a long sigh. "I'm the one who talked you into this in the first place."

"Really, Terra, it's no biggie." She could tell Terra felt horrible about the situation but it certainly wasn't her fault. How was she to have known that Dr. Dipshit was going to be there?

"What are you going to do now?"

"I think I'll just head on home."

"You want me to come with you? We could open a couple of bottles of wine and continue to thoroughly trash the good doc."

Jess couldn't help but laugh. "As tempting as that sounds, I think I'd rather just be by myself."

Terra leaned in. "You sure? I'm more than willing to come hang out."

"Yes, I'm sure but thanks." Actually, she had some plans of her own. Nothing would work off her frustration like a good run in her racing chair or some handcycling, anything to give her a hard workout and take her mind off things.

"Okay." Terra patted her on the back. "Just don't let it get to you. If you need anything..."

"Yeah, you'll be the first I call."

With that, Terra turned and jogged across the street to her parked car. Jess continued to smile. With friends like Terra, she could get through anything, even insensitive jerks like Dr. Alex.

Still, it was hard not to fume about idiots like that. How would they do living just one day in her shoes? As Terra pulled away from the curb honking her horn, Jess gripped her wheels and with a good forward thrust, quickly rolled down the street and around the corner.

* * *

Alex clapped her hands to her mouth while everyone around the table continued to stare at her. "Oh my God, I can't believe that just happened." It had been like a horrible car accident, everything unraveling in slow motion yet she could only sit there stunned, unable to move a muscle. But now that the initial shock had worn off, it felt as if someone had pushed fast-forward. Einstein was right—time really was relative. As the full weight of what she had done finally registered, she leaped up from the table. "I've got to go. I need to find her and apologize."

She didn't wait for a response but hustled out the front doors. When she hit the street, she quickly looked in both directions, hoping upon hope to catch sight of the woman she had just insulted. Even though it had been unintentional, that was no excuse. Laziness? Had she really said that? No wonder the girl left pissed. In her place, she would've done the same. Actually, she was surprised that she hadn't thrown something at her first—a glass, a chair, hell even the table. Lord knows she would've deserved it. But Jess was nowhere in sight. "Damn."

With nothing else to do, Alex slowly turned and shuffled back inside. Jamie quickly whirled around. "Did you catch her?"

"No." With a deep sigh, her shoulders dropped. She quickly pulled out a twenty and threw it into the center. "Hey, I'm going to take off."

"Are you sure? You're more than welcome to stay."

"Yeah, I'm going to head home before I make more of an ass of myself."

"It wasn't *that* bad." Jamie bit her bottom lip.

"Come on, Jamie, you can't be serious. You heard what I said. If that's not bad, I don't know what is." Alex raised her

eyebrows and gave her a wry twist of lips. It couldn't exactly be called a smile, more like a nauseous grimace.

Jamie winced. "Okay, yeah it *was* that bad but hey, tomorrow's another day, right?"

"That's what they say." If only she could believe it herself.

Jamie gave her a strong, heartfelt hug. She finally pulled back and turned to the table. "Sorry for…" She absently waved her hand beside her face. What could she say? "Sorry for that."

There was the low murmur around the table, a general consensus of "don't worry about it" and "no big deal." But it didn't sound genuine. Sue jumped up and clapped her on the back. "Hey, it'll all work out." As she shuffled back out, she hoped Sue was right but damned if she knew how.

Even later, as she lay awake, the clock ticking loudly on the wall, she still couldn't shake it. This had to be one of her all-time worst days ever. Her rudeness, cruelty and contempt weren't like her. Or maybe, working for years in the ER had turned her a lot more bitter and cynical than she had realized. That alone was a horrible thought. Had she really become so hardened and numb that she could no longer distinguish between people truly with a need and those who merely tried to work the system? Had it all blurred into one pale shade of gray? She shuddered as she stared up into the darkness. Was she that burned out?

If she could only get some sleep. She had been up for thirty-six, forty hours straight? Every part of her was exhausted. But every time she closed her eyes, she could still see the look on Jess's face—not so much a look of anger, although there was certainly enough of that there, but more a look of hurt, a look of pain. She was going to have to do something. First thing tomorrow. It would be sooner if she could. She'd have gone right then if she knew how to find her. Then again, if she showed up at Jess's door in the middle of night, the girl would probably call the police, not that she would blame her. With that thought, she finally smiled and rolled over onto her side. Yes, first thing tomorrow.

CHAPTER TWO

"Hey, look what I've got." Terra sidled up with a cup of coffee in each hand, handing one to Jess as she worked at the Espresso Book Machine. She was printing out the books for the Kent District Library short story contest.

"Java! You're a real lifesaver." Jess took a sip, holding the cup under her nose and deeply inhaling the pungent aroma.

Sipping their coffee, they sat in silence. Terra finally lowered her cup and leaned forward tentatively. "So, how are you doing this morning?"

Jess waved toward the Espresso Book Machine busy churning out copies. "We're doing pretty good here. If all goes well, I should have this run completed this morning—that'll really please Kendra down at KDL—and then I can get started on that self-pub job." She didn't meet Terra's eyes.

"That's all good news but you *know* that wasn't what I was asking." Terra gave Jess a wry smile. "So level with me, how are you doing this morning—you know, after yesterday and all?"

"I'm fine." Jess finally looked over at Terra, at the deep concern on her face, and sighed. "Seriously, I'm fine."

"I just worry about you, you know that."

"Yes I do and I appreciate that. But it's nothing I haven't heard before. One thing about the chair, you learn very quick to develop a pretty thick skin." She couldn't count the times she had repeated that over the years—*you learn very quick to develop a pretty thick skin.* It was a mantra. Still, it wasn't easy and if she were completely honest, for some reason the encounter had stung more than usual. But she didn't want Terra to worry. Like she had said, it's nothing she hadn't heard before and sadly wouldn't hear again.

"Well, just don't develop so thick a skin that you forget to let your friends in."

"I won't." Jess cleared her throat. Leave it to Terra to choke her up. But that's what made her such a good friend. Terra saw her for herself, not just a girl in a chair.

"Good." Terra stood and clapped her on the back. "I'd better get back to that huge promotional display I'm supposed to put together or I might get the ax."

"Like that's ever going to happen. Of anyone, you have total job security."

"What, just because my parents own the place? You think they wouldn't fire their own daughter?" Terra flashed a mischievous little grin.

Laughing, Jess nearly spilled her coffee. This was one of their favorite games—how to get fired, an ongoing joke. Bob and Liz were actually wonderful bosses. They had both gone out of their way to welcome Jess into not only the business, making sure that everything was wheelchair-accessible throughout the entire complex, but also welcomed her into their family like a second daughter. So when they talk about getting fired, it was always tongue-in-cheek. "I'd better get back to printing these books or *I* might get fired."

"Please…" Terra drew the word out. "Talk about job security—you could burn the store down and they still wouldn't fire you."

As Terra trotted away, Jess shook her head and turned back to the Espresso Book Machine, busy churning out yet another book. Terra was absolutely correct—she probably *could* burn the store down and not get fired. That was how Bob and Liz were, the picture of compassion and understanding. They went out of their way to try to make life easier for her, for which she was eternally grateful. Yet at the same time, they didn't do it in a patronizing way that made her feel helpless or—well, there just wasn't any other way to put—*disabled*. Sadly, people like that were rare, as evidenced by the disaster with the bitch yesterday. If anyone could use a lesson in compassion and understanding, it was certainly her.

* * *

Alex stumbled bleary-eyed into the shower and turned the water on full blast. She'd had a grand total of one hour—two tops—of sleep all night. Every muscle in her body ached. Her head pounded. Her stomach churned. Overall, she simply felt like crap. Hopefully she would soon be able to remedy that.

She stood there, holding herself up with one arm against the side of the shower, the steaming water pouring over her head. With her eyes closed, she quickly scrubbed her body. Finally, she turned the water all way over to cold, hoping that might blast some vigor into her. Didn't help. All it gave her was a wicked case of the shivers and motivated her to jump out of the shower. She grabbed a towel and dabbed herself dry then wiped the steam from the mirror. She leaned in, closer, closer, taking in her appearance. "Yikes." Not only did she feel like crap, she looked like crap. The circles under her eyes couldn't be darker if she had painted them there with a can of Krylon. And her eyes—talk about bloodshot. There was more red than white. If only she could crawl back in bed, but that would be of no use, not until she could at least offer an apology to Jess.

Alex walked naked to her bedroom where she grabbed a comfy pair of jeans and a short sleeved, black silk blouse. A blouse might seem a bit overdressed, but on her days off, it

felt good to wear anything but scrubs. She quickly got a cup of coffee brewing in her Keurig. If anything was going to get her through the day, it would be coffee. She picked up her cell and dialed Jamie. Jamie would know for sure how she could get in contact with Jess.

On the third ring, Jamie picked up. "Hey, you're up early."

Alex glanced at the clock on the stove. Ten fifteen—not that early but definitely early for her. On her days off, it was a miracle if she crawled out of bed before noon. "Yeah, I didn't sleep well last night."

"You didn't stay up all night worrying about what happened yesterday, did you?"

Alex could hear the concern in Jamie's voice. She knew her well. "Sort of. That's actually why I'm calling—you wouldn't know how I could get hold of that Jess, would you?"

"Why? Are you thinking about going to talk to her?"

"That was the idea. Try to apologize for being such an idiot."

Jamie laughed on the other end. "Well, I guess it couldn't hurt. She works with Terra at Infinity Books. You can probably catch her there."

"Great. I think I'll go over there, try to set things right."

"Good luck, Alex. Call me later and tell me how it goes."

"Will do." Alex paused. "And hey, thanks a ton, Jamie."

"Anytime hon. Anytime."

Alex closed her eyes and took a long deep breath, slowly rubbing her temples. At least her headache had faded to a mild throbbing. Maybe the shower had done some good. Either that or talking to Jamie. She quickly grabbed her travel mug of coffee, dumped in five teaspoons of sugar, grabbed her keys and headed out the door. The sooner she got this over with, the better.

* * *

"Hey, Jess."

Jess smashed the back of her head on the frame of the Espresso Book Machine as she was feeding in a ream of paper.

Her heart thundered in her chest. "Thanks a lot, Terra." She sat up, rubbing the back of her head, a lump already forming.

"Sorry about that." Terra cringed. "Just to give you a heads-up, that doctor from yesterday just walked in the front door."

"What? You've got to be kidding." Jess wheeled herself back, craning her neck to see the front of the store. Sure enough, she could make out Alex stepping up in front of the information desk. "What the hell is she doing here?"

Terra shrugged as she leaned against the book machine. "Don't know. Crazy thought—maybe she's here to buy a book."

"She should get one on how not to be a dick."

Terra chuckled. "True. Very true. And at the same time she could pick up *one hundred and one ways to stop being a bitch*."

Jess joined Terra laughing. They were probably being a little too catty but the good doctor pretty much deserved it. Just then, Kaylee, who was working behind the information desk, leaned over the counter and pointed directly toward them. Alex followed her finger, gave a quick nod and set off in their direction. "Oh shit, don't look now. Here she comes."

"This can't be good."

Terra didn't need to say that twice.

Alex walked up, her head hanging. She took a deep breath. "Can I talk to you for a moment please, Jess?" She glanced from Jess to Terra from whom she received a "die bitch die" look. She quickly turned back to Jess and added, "Maybe alone."

Terra continued to glare, her arms crossed. "I think anything you've got to say can be said in front of both of us."

Jess smiled at Terra's protectiveness. As mild-mannered and soft-spoken as Terra usually was, she looked as if she were about two seconds away from tearing the doctor's arm off and beating her with it, which had its own appeal. "It's okay, Terra. I've got this." With that, she spun around and rolled herself toward the studio, leaving it up to Alex to follow. She whipped around and waited there, not saying a word.

Alex paused, shuffling her feet. Finally she lowered her eyes and cleared her throat. "First, I'd like to say how sorry I am about what I said yesterday. It was appalling. I know it's no

excuse, but I was having a bad day and shot my mouth off. I never meant to hurt you, which I obviously did. You have every right to be pissed at me."

Jess was taken aback. She would have thought it more likely that the good doctor would have tried to find some justification to rationalize what she had said but that didn't seem to be the case. Alex seemed genuinely contrite. "Oh…okay. We all make mistakes." Her voice flat, Jess wasn't going to let her guard down, not yet. Not until she knew Alex's true intentions. It was equally likely she had caught hell from her friends and was now trying to make up for it.

"Again, I am really sorry. If there's anything, anything at all, I can do to make it up to you, please, please let me know. Could we start over?"

Jess met Alex's eyes, an intense light blue, almost an azure. She was just about to wave her off when it occurred to her—if Alex *was* sincere, there was something she could do. "What are you doing Saturday?"

"Nothing, I'm off. Why?"

"If you're serious, there *is* something you can do."

"Anything, just name it."

"If you really want to make it up to me, there's a 5K run downtown on Saturday to benefit disabled kids. I seem to remember you saying something about running fifteen miles a week so this shouldn't be any problem. If you can keep up with me, that is."

"I'll be there."

Jess merely nodded. She wasn't sure if she should believe Alex or not. The doctor might just be blowing smoke. Still, she would see come Saturday. She whirled around, leaving Alex standing in the middle of the studio. As she wheeled away, she called back over her shoulder. "Starts at noon. Don't be late."

Terra was waiting for her at the Espresso Book Machine. She quickly leaned in. "What the hell did she want?" If Terra's tone could kill, it would've taken out a small city.

"She was here to apologize. Said she wanted to make it up to me."

"You told her to kiss your butt, right?"

"Oh, I did one better. Told her she could make it up by doing the 5K benefit with me. We'll see if she is as good a runner as she boasts—if she even appears." Part of her had doubts Alex would show but another part of her hoped she would. Let her try to keep up with her. She would find out just how good a runner she was indeed.

* * *

Alex felt a little better as she stepped out of the bookstore. It may not have been the warmest of receptions but at least Jess had heard her out. Maybe now she could clear her mind and get a little sleep. But first, she jumped behind the wheel of her car and pulled out her cell, ready to give Jamie a call before heading home. But it was just too nice a day for that. It was hard to think about sleeping when it was eighty degrees and sunny. Thinking better of it, she tossed her cell on the passenger seat and pulled out into the busy traffic on Twenty-eighth Street.

Twenty-five minutes later, she pulled into the Monroe Center parking ramp across from the Grand Rapids Art Museum, where Jamie worked as the associate curator. She hopped out and ran across the street. She took the steps two at a time, burst through the front doors and hustled up to the ticket counter.

"Hey Lois, is Jamie in?" She had visited Jamie frequently enough to know most of the staff on a first name basis.

Lois looked up from her newspaper puzzle. Silver-haired and in her late seventies, Lois embodied the Norman Rockwell image of the perfect grandmother. The only thing missing was an apron around her waist and a tin of fresh-baked cookies. "Alex, so good to see you. I just saw Jamie a few minutes ago so I know she's floating around here. She's probably either in her office or down in the acquisitions room. They just got a new exhibit so I know everyone's pretty excited about that. Why don't you go on back."

Alex smiled at the older woman's sweetness. "Thanks Lois. Good luck on your word search."

Lois laughed, soft and warm. "You're such a darling. You know at my age, every little bit helps to keep the mind sharp."

Alex flashed Lois another smile before turning away. Lois had the sharpest mind of any older person she knew and it was probably no coincidence that she was rarely spotted without a book, a puzzle, Sudoku or anything else that would exercise her mind. Study after study showed an active mind is a healthy mind and Lois was proof of just that. Hopefully her mind would age as gracefully.

Alex clopped up the stairs to the offices. Most visitors never got to see this part of the museum. She walked down the hall and poked her head into Jamie's office, but she wasn't there. She could wait for her there but more likely, as Lois had said, she was probably downstairs. Sure enough, as she poked her head into the large holding area, Jamie immediately yelled out, "Alex! What a surprise." She hustled over and threw her arms around Alex. "I thought you said you were going to call when you got done meeting with Jess."

Alex returned Jamie's hug with a quick kiss on her cheek. "I was, but it's such a nice day I was wondering if I could tempt you to lunch."

"You know I don't need any coaxing when it comes to lunch, as all my pants seem to show." Jamie patted her nonexistent belly.

"Whatever." Alex rolled her eyes. She'd give anything to have Jamie's supposed problem with tight-fitting clothes. The girl was a walking toothpick. It was hard not to be jealous. If she didn't exercise constantly and run at least three times a week, not to mention watch everything she ate, she quickly found herself battling a good ten, fifteen extra pounds. That's how she'd started running in the first place.

Jamie flashed a wide, bright smile. It wasn't anything that hadn't been said before. "Give me just a second and then we can take off."

Alex leaned against the door as Jamie quickly gave a long set of instructions to the team opening the exhibits. She trotted over and grabbed Alex by the hand. "There, they should be able to handle it for a while. What do you say to Mediterranean?"

"Works for me."

They walked across the street to the Parsley Mediterranean Grill where Jamie grabbed a tabouli salad—no wonder she was so thin—while Alex opted for a hummus fattoush wrap with feta. She probably didn't need the feta but what the hell, it was a nice day. They both chose a Turkish coffee and settled into a table near the window where they could watch the cars zipping up and down Ottawa.

Jamie took a big bite of her salad before she leaned over, dabbing her lips with a napkin. "So, how did it go with Jess?"

Alex covered her mouth with her hand as she choked down a huge bite of her wrap. "Not too bad, I guess." She bobbed her head side to side.

"That's good at least. I still can't believe you said what you said. How could you not see that she was in a wheelchair? You of all people!"

"I swear I couldn't. It was dark and she has one of those sporty wheelchairs with a small back so from where I was sitting, it just looked like any old chair. Talk about one of my all-time biggest screw-ups. Chalk it up to bad lighting and working a double shift. I couldn't figure out why everyone was looking at me so oddly and Sue kept kicking me under the table."

Jamie burst out laughing. "Did she really? She didn't tell me that."

"I have the bruises to prove it."

"That's so Sue. I've had my fair share of kicks under the table. So tell me, what did Jess have to say?"

"Not too much really. She took it all right—a lot better than her friend. She's still pretty angry with me." She blew out a low whistle.

"From what little I know of Terra, she is pretty protective of her friends. Hopefully this will clear the air with everyone in the Lesbian Professionals of West Michigan group. We need everyone we can get."

"Next time I think I'll just sit there and keep my mouth shut—that is if there is a next time."

"We all make mistakes." Jamie waved her off. "If someone can't understand that, then maybe they aren't right to be leading this group. We all need to work together and support the community."

Alex took a quick sip of her coffee. "Speaking of supporting the community, Jess wants me to enter a benefit run for disabled children this Saturday as a way of atoning."

"There you go." Jamie reached out and patted Alex's hand. "That's what we need to do, put our differences aside and all come together in support of each other. This is great."

Alex smiled and shook her head as she watched the fire in Jamie's eyes and heard the passion in her voice. She wasn't sure when Jamie had become such a community activist. Maybe Jamie had always been that way but she was only noticing it now. And all the time that Alex had known her, Jamie had never met a cause that she didn't embrace. It was a wonder poor Sue could keep up, but she was nearly as enthusiastic and in that way, they were perfect for each other. If only she were so lucky. But when it came to romance, she was a disaster. Long hours in a demanding job and an unpredictable schedule didn't help. "I guess it's the least I can do."

"How many times have I told you, you need to get out more?"

"What are you talking about? I get out all the time. I run and work out, and then there's you and Sue. What more do I need?"

"Alex, Alex, Alex…" Jamie shook her head. "That's not what I mean and you know it. You need to socialize more, network and connect. And not just when I drag you out. You don't want to become some crazy old cat lady."

"What are you talking about? I don't have a cat."

"I know that." Jamie again laid her hand on Alex's, this time a mischievous little glint in her eye. "And sweetie, that's the only reason I'm not more worried about you."

Alex guffawed. One of Jamie's favorite pastimes had to be picking on her but it was all in good fun. And like Jamie said, it probably wouldn't hurt for her to get out and socialize more.

* * *

Jess rolled through the door to her physical therapist at six minutes past three. She was concerned that she wouldn't make it, having lost track of time at work. Alex's unexpected visit hadn't helped either. Still, neither would have been a problem if she hadn't had to leave work two hours early for this appointment. She didn't like to complain—life was too short for that—but it was sometimes a huge pain in the butt. There were more than a few things about the chair that were irritating—physical therapy, catheters, sanctimonious bigoted idiots. She laughed at the last one. At least *that* one had made an effort to apologize. Saturday would show how sincere was her remorse.

Jerome, her physical therapist called out, "Hey girlfriend. How's my little sis doing today?" At nearly six foot, he always reminded her of a blend of Samuel L. Jackson, Will Smith, and RuPaul. On the weekends he was also a regular drag performer. That's where she had first met him and they'd been friends ever since.

"Not too bad here, Jerome. And you?"

"Honey, I'm doing better now just since you walked in." He bobbed his head in the most flamboyant way imaginable.

Jerome's personality did as much for her spirits as the actual physical therapy did for her body. With his other patients he had to tone it down but for her it was different. As he liked to point out, they were family. "You're the biggest flatterer, Jerome."

"You know it, girl. How about we go see how you're doing?"

With that, Jess rolled down the hall to the physical therapy room where she slipped out of her chair and heaved herself up on the table. She stretched out, lying on her back. Jerome stepped up beside her and began kneading the muscles in her right leg. Even though she had had it done hundreds of times, she still found it disconcerting that she couldn't feel her legs being massaged. It was the strangest sensation—she might not be able to feel the actual touch in her leg but as Jerome worked back and forth, that little movement subtly transferred up her

leg, through her hips, and to her upper body where she most definitely could feel it. Difficult to explain.

Jerome switched to her left leg. "Have you been doing your exercises at home?"

"Of course." Not exactly one hundred percent the truth, but what could she say? She had been busy.

"Ah huh." Jerome pursed his lips. "Now you know I can tell when you're lying to me."

Busted. "All right, I've had a lot to do lately and haven't gotten around to it."

Jerome now worked her leg through its full range of motion, stretching the muscles. "I understand that sweetie, but this needs to be at the top of your priority list. Trust me, you don't want muscle atrophy and contracture, not with these beautiful legs."

Jess let out a long sigh. "I know, I know." Jerome was absolutely right. Ever since she had lost the use of her legs, she had heard the importance of continual stretching and exercise of the affected limb. It seemed silly at first—what was the big deal if her muscles atrophied if she could never use them again? But then she had heard the horror stories, the threats of multiple surgeries, and that had pretty much convinced her. But it could be a real pain. Therapy, rehab, exercise, therapy, rehab, exercise—sometimes it felt as if that was all her life had become. "I'll work a bit harder from now on."

Jerome switched to her other leg. "Promise?"

"Yes, I promise."

Forty-five minutes later, Jess slipped behind the wheel of her car and headed home. She lived ten miles north of Grand Rapids in Rockford. She would've preferred to be closer to Grand Rapids but she had fallen in love with her little house. She had been lucky to find it—wheelchair-accessible and right next to the White Pine Trail State Park, the old turn-of-the-century Grand Rapids and Indiana railroad. It had been converted into a paved walking, running, biking trail that ran all the way south of Rockford to Comstock Park and all the way north to Cadillac, covering over ninety-three miles through five counties. She couldn't pass that up. What better way to get exercise, whether training in her racing chair or her handcycle?

Pulling into her garage, she glanced out the side window of her car at her custom-built racing wheelchair. It had cost as much as a good used car but thanks to the gang at Infinity Books, they had held a big fundraiser that paid for most of it. Same with her handcycle and the hand control conversion for her car. Without the support of friends and family, not to mention a fair share of generous strangers, she wouldn't have been able to afford any of it. It was difficult for her. Before her accident, she had been independent and self-reliant. Then in an instant, she was anything but. Probably the biggest lesson she had learned from it all was humility.

Jess opened her door and wrestled her chair from the backseat. She had planned to kick back the rest of the night and relax, maybe catch a movie on cable, but it was too nice an evening for that. She wheeled herself into the house and changed into her shorts and jersey she wore when working out with her racing chair. Usually a twenty-minute task, she completed everything in record time and fifteen minutes later she was rolling out of her garage and onto the trail.

She paced herself heading south out of Rockford, limbering up her arm and shoulder muscles. There was a lot of foot traffic in town, which was hardly surprising on such a perfect early summer evening. But as soon as the pedestrians thinned out, she picked up speed, pushing harder and harder, feeling the perfect fluid motion of her muscles working together. The wind whistled past her ears as she went faster and faster. She could almost forget she couldn't use her legs. With her heart hammering, she felt utterly alive, unimpaired. It had to be one of the greatest feelings ever.

* * *

Alex slowed her pace, fighting the stitch in her side. She had been pushing herself a little too much, but after agreeing to run in the benefit that weekend, she figured she'd better step up her game. Last thing she wanted was to look like a total idiot in front of everyone, especially after she had already shot off her

mouth. Not one of her finer moments. Maybe this Saturday she could make up for that.

Her stitch was fading. She sucked in deep breath after deep breath and stretched out her stride again. Her feet hit the pavement with a steady *swat, swat, swat*. Every muscle in her legs worked to propel her forward—quads, hamstrings, hip flexors, calf muscles, all the way up through her glutes. All the muscles throughout her entire body worked in big and small ways. She hadn't really thought about it like that before. She had simply run. But what would happen if suddenly she couldn't do that anymore? What would happen if those muscles no longer worked? Could she see herself confined to a chair? Like most people, she had never given it a moment's thought, but for Jess, it was her life. It would be so hard not to be bitter.

The more she thought about the benefit run, the more excited she became. She wasn't sure why. Sure, it would be a way to make it up to Jess for being an insensitive jerk but there was more to it than that. Since the incident in the restaurant, she couldn't take her mind off Jess. The nagging sense of shame and guilt. But even after apologizing, her thoughts kept returning to the woman. Her heartbeat sped up even more. Maybe the road had just picked up an incline. Either way, one thing was for sure—for some reason she just couldn't get Jess out of her mind.

CHAPTER THREE

Jess sat in her racing chair and flexed her hands in her black leather fingerless gloves, stretching before the race. She limbered each shoulder by stretching her long, wiry arms behind her head. Runners warmed up by stretching their legs. She warmed up by stretching her arms and shoulders. Just one of the differences with life in the chair. She could feel her heartbeat picking up as she waited. Less than ten minutes to the start. She was registered, she had her bib, she was ready to go. The only thing left was a blast from the starter pistol.

"Is there anything you need?" Terra knelt down beside her.

"Nope, I'm all set." Jess worked at controlling her breathing, part of her pre-race routine. "You know, Terra, you should try running sometime. Might be good for you."

Terra shook her head, sending her white dreads flying. "I don't think so. I get winded just going up the steps to my apartment. If I tried running, I'd probably have a heart attack."

"That's why you should go running...or at least some sort of exercise."

"I get plenty just walking around the bookstore. Plus there's no way I could ever keep up with you. You're a speed demon."

"You know it." Jess spun her arms around in a wide arc, continuing to loosen up. The race would begin any minute.

Terra turned and scanned the crowd. "Doesn't look like the good doctor showed." She pursed her lips.

Jess rolled her eyes. Why wasn't she surprised? "Figures. Did you really expect her to?"

"I don't know…I guess I figured she might since she went out of her way to come and apologize."

Jess snorted. She had thought the same thing. Why make that effort and not follow through? Just went the show how sincere Alex had really been. "You know, who cares? It's not like it's a great loss."

"I don't believe it!" Terra gasped.

"What's not to believe? She obviously—"

Terra quickly slapped her on her arm to get her attention. "No, no, she's here."

Jess whirled around in her chair. "Well I'll be…" Sure enough, Alex was walking toward them through the crowd, dressed in formfitting black and neon green running shorts and a matching tank, a racing bib plastered to her chest.

Alex stepped up beside her with a shrug, a sheepish grin lifting her lips. "I made it."

"I see that. No unworthy handicapped people poaching parking spaces?"

"Okay, I deserved that." Alex's sheepish grin quickly turned to a full-on wry smile. "Just so you know, I parked five blocks away and never once complained."

"There's hope for you yet." Jess gave a firm nod. She didn't know why but she was rather enjoying dishing it out. Alex had made a mistake—so she said. She could accept that and Alex sure seemed to be making good on her promise. Still that wasn't going to prevent her from giving her a bit more crap.

Alex turned to Terra, offering her a wide smile.

Terra glared back. From the set of her shoulders and the thin line of her lips, Terra was no closer to forgiving Alex. The girl could hold a grudge.

Alex's smile quickly faded into a wince as she turned back to Jess and leaned in close. "Apparently I've got a ways to go yet to win over your friend."

"Don't mind Terra. She's harmless—really." Jess winked at Terra for which she received a Terra scowl. Jess knew Terra was a sweetheart, but it was going to take a little time and more than a little luck before she looked at Alex without a murderous glint in her eye.

The announcement for starting positions rang out.

Terra wrapped her arm around Jess's shoulders. "I'll be waiting for you at the finish line." She shot another filthy look at Alex before walking away.

Alex sucked in a quick breath. "So this is it?"

"Yep, this is it."

"Just to let you know, this is my first time running in a race. Should I hold back and run along beside you?"

"*Hold back?*" Jess quickly whipped her head around. Was this woman kidding? Then she noticed the smirk on Alex's lips. "Just see if you can keep up, Legs."

* * *

At the sound of the starter pistol, Alex kicked off smiling. It seemed that she had finally broken the ice with Jess. A bit of a risk with her joke but it had paid off. Or so she thought. Jess took off in her chair like a monkey out of a box and it was all she could do to catch her.

She huffed along, her heart pounding. This was a much faster pace than she was used to but she wasn't going to slow down. Beside her, Jess zipped along, her arms and shoulders pumping away. She couldn't believe how fast she was going. Somehow in her mind she had always equated "wheelchair" with "slow." Jess was anything but. She was having a hell of a time keeping up.

But as she watched her out of the corner of her eye, she couldn't help but appreciate Jess's fluid movements. It was a far cry better than her clomping along. Compared to Jess, she felt like a baby giraffe trying to run in high heels.

"How're you doing over there, Legs?"

"Just fine here," she gasped between breaths. "What about you?"

"Nice easy pace."

Nice easy pace, her aching glutes, but Alex wasn't about to admit that. She was going to keep up with her at all costs. "Yep, just a Sunday stroll."

"In that case, let's pick it up a bit."

Great. That'd teach her for being a smartass. Alex kicked forward with all the strength in her legs, which were quickly turning to rubber. Her breath seared her lungs like fire. She concentrated on each footstep hitting the pavement. *You can do this, you can do this*—she repeated that over and over in her head. She couldn't ever remember being in such agony but she'd be damned if she let up now.

It wasn't long before they found themselves alone, only the two of them. The large crowd of runners had spread out, a few dozen in front of them, but the vast majority had fallen behind. Alex couldn't remember ever running this fast in her life. Sure, a 5K was the distance running equivalent of a sprint, but this was ridiculous. From the corner of her eye, she could see Jess, sweat running down the side of her face and arms as she pushed herself along. Her white tank with blue striping clung to her body as if she had just rolled through a car wash. Alex knew she couldn't look much better. She felt as if she had showered in her clothes, except at least that would have felt refreshing. Still, she kept pace beside Jess. If Jess could do it, so could she.

* * *

Jess could feel the palms of her hands burning through her leather gloves. Fun was fun but as she glanced over at Alex, she eased up. Alex's face was a bit blotchy as she huffed along. She was still sweating so Jess wasn't too concerned. Now if she wasn't sweating, that would be a different story. She knew all too well the dangers of heat exhaustion. It had crept up on her more than once. One of the things she had learned early on

after her accident was that athletes with spinal cord injuries have an impaired ability to regulate their core temperature. Vasomotor and sudomotor activity is compromised below the level of injury.

Still, she was impressed by Alex's performance. The doctor was admirably tenacious. Even so, she didn't want to run her until she dropped.

"How you doing over there, Legs?"

"Fine…just fine, Wheels." Alex yelled back through gritted teeth.

Jess laughed. *Wheels?* That was as fitting a nickname as anything, especially after she had been calling Alex *Legs* all afternoon. Fair was fair. Plus if Alex was joking with her, it meant she was beginning to see her beyond the chair.

"We're well over the halfway point. Not much farther."

"Fucking terrific," Alex mumbled under her breath.

"What was that, Legs?"

"Nothing…nothing at all."

Jess fought hard not to laugh. She had to give it to the girl. Alex was certainly being a sport, even if she looked as if she were in utter agony. When the starter pistol had gone off, she hadn't expected Alex to make it a kilometer in, especially at this pace, but here they were coming up on the four-kilometer point and she was still hoofing it along. There was no other way to put it—she was impressed.

She knew she was coming up on that dreaded point of the race—The Wall. It was the point where every "step" felt as if it were uphill, even when going downhill. Or more precisely for her, when her arms and shoulders felt as if they had turned to lead. If she was feeling this exhausted, Alex had to be much worse. For all of Alex's earlier bluster about running fifteen miles every week, a casual run and a competitive race were two entirely different creatures. So if she was hitting the wall, Alex must've already plowed into it headfirst. Jess glanced over at her. It looked as if the wall had fallen over on top of her. Yet she kept going.

They rounded the last corner, the finish line only three blocks away. Alex looked as if she were about to drop any moment now. Jess couldn't help but feel for her. Talk about determination.

"You're almost there, Legs. You can do it."

Alex didn't reply, only nodded and gasped along.

They finished one block. The crowd along the sides of the street cheered them on but for Jess, it was only so much background noise. The only thing she was focused on was Alex and her own determination to finish. Her hands burned, her arms burned, her shoulders burned—hell, even her eyes burned.

They finished the second block. Alex was still right beside her. "Come on, Legs, you've got this. Don't give up now."

"Only a little farther...only a little farther..." Alex kept gasping out the words, over and over, staring straight ahead.

Only a hundred meters now...then fifty...then twenty—they were almost there. Ten meters...five meters...they crossed the line. Alex collapsed on her hands and knees and rolled onto her side just past the finish line. Volunteers and medics immediately raced over. Jess stopped beside her, doubled over and gasping. Someone handed her a water bottle. She took a massive drink then poured the rest over her head. By now, Alex was sitting up, drinking from her own water bottle.

"You did it!" Jess was deeply impressed. Alex had given it her all to the point that once across the finish line, her body had collapsed.

Alex simply nodded while she gasped, still sipping water while volunteers covered her with towels. Someone threw a towel over her shoulders. Just then Terra ran up.

"Are you all right? You look terrible." Her genuine concern was evident.

"Yeah, I'm fine. Just got a little carried away."

Three volunteers were helping Alex to her feet. Her legs trembled as she stood.

Terra stared. "Oh man, the good doctor looks half dead. What did you do, try to run her to death?"

Alex looked over with a wide, almost crazed, smile on her lips.

"No, she's good." Jess thrust out her fist and knuckle bumped Alex. "Aren't you, Legs?"

"Never better, Wheels."

The volunteers and medics didn't seem to be as confident as Alex. They remained around her, worried that she would tip over again. Slowly, they walked with her to the med tent. Jess rolled beside her, Terra pushing her along. She couldn't have pushed herself if she'd tried. It was all she could do to simply hold her water bottle. She couldn't remember the last time someone had given her such a run for her money.

Once under the tent, Alex flopped down in a chair, taking a long drink. Terra rolled Jess up beside her. She glanced over at Alex and when their eyes met, they both began to laugh. There was a note of craziness in their laughter. "Good race, Legs."

Alex threw her arm around her shoulders. "Yes, good race, Wheels."

* * *

Sunday afternoon, Alex was lying flat on her back on her couch listening to NPR on the radio. She had overdone it and she was paying for it now. She should have known better. The human body could only take so much. It had limits—she had limits. But had she listened to them? Absolutely not. She was going to keep up with Jess at all costs.

Every muscle in her body hurt—every bone, every ligament, every tendon, every flipping cell hurt. She could safely say that she had never hurt as much in her entire life. If she had rolled down every single flight of stairs at the hospital, she wouldn't feel as bad. For crying out loud, it even hurt to blink. But at the same time, she couldn't be prouder of herself. She still wasn't quite sure how she had done it but somehow she had finished that race—and in fifth place! Actually, she had Jess to thank for that. She wouldn't have finished the last few blocks if it hadn't been for her encouragement. As good as completing the race had felt, she was paying for it today.

Just as *This American Life* was finishing, someone knocked on the front door. Alex tried to sit up but as her whole body

cried out, she collapsed back on the couch. Instead she cupped her hand to her mouth and called out. "Just come on in."

Whoever it was, knocked again. Probably a salesperson or Girl Scouts selling cookies. The latter sounded good. She could do with two, three…or maybe even ten boxes at the moment. She took a deep breath and called out again. "The door's open, come on in."

Again, a knock rang out. This was turning into a bad joke, like some sort of crazed Abbott and Costello routine. *Who's at the door? Who? Who's on the couch. Well, if who's on the couch then what's that at the door? What? Yeah. I don't know. I don't know's at the window*…Alex rolled onto her side and with all she could muster, yelled out. "For the love of God, the door's open so just come on in already!"

The door finally opened and Jamie poked in her head. "Hey there you are. Why didn't you answer the door?"

"Oh, I don't know…maybe because I can barely move."

Jamie walked in and sat down on the corner of the coffee table in front of Alex. "Here I was going to ask you how the race went yesterday but from the looks of it, I'd say you may have overdone it a bit." She held up her hand with her thumb and index finger half an inch apart.

"You don't say? What could *possibly* give you that idea?" Alex shot Jamie a sarcastic wry grin.

"Oh I don't know…maybe the fact that you look like death warmed over. I'm not kidding, I saw a road-killed raccoon on my way over here that looked in better shape than you."

"Nice." All Alex could do was roll her eyes and even that hurt. "Instead of laughing at me, how about helping me sit up?"

Jamie grabbed both of Alex's hands and heaved. "Man, you really *did* overdo it."

Now sitting upright, Alex leaned back into the couch. Her legs throbbed. "Tell me about it. I felt just fine yesterday but when I woke up this morning, I could barely move. I had to crawl out here to the couch."

Jamie laughed again and sat down beside her. "All I can say, Alex, is when you do something, you do it up."

"Is there any other way?"

"Maybe not trying to kill yourself. What were you thinking anyway?"

Jamie had her there. What *had* she been thinking? Why had she pushed herself so hard? Sure, she had always had a competitive streak. She was a doctor after all and you certainly couldn't be that without knowing how to push yourself. But this had gone beyond that—way beyond that. She shifted her weight, trying her best to find some way to sit that didn't hurt. Finally, she gave it up as a lost cause. "I'm not really sure what I was thinking, Jamie. I guess I wasn't."

"Let me guess—you were running with Jess and you weren't going to quit no matter what, even if you dropped dead of a heart attack. How am I doing so far?"

"I wasn't quite that bad."

"Says the girl sitting on her couch unable to move." Jamie eyed her a bit more intensely, a wide smile lifting her lips. "So, does Jess know?"

"Does Jess know what?"

"That you like her."

"I...um...no idea...I mean...well...she's okay I guess?" She could feel her face growing warm.

"Okay you guess? Please. You can't fool me, Alex. You really like Jess or you wouldn't have nearly killed yourself trying to keep up with her."

"Ah...ah...I have no idea what you're talking about." Even to Alex, it sounded like an out-and-out lie.

"Come on, Alex. You've always been the same. The more you like someone, the more competitive you seem to become. Need I remind you of Becky?"

Alex didn't need reminding. That relationship had been a total disaster, mostly of her own doing. They were both highly competitive and everything between them was a contest. At first, it had been fun but as time went on, her competitive spirit had taken over until they became more adversaries than lovers. The sex had been great. There was no denying that. Heated, passionate, intense. But that wasn't enough. They couldn't be

great in the bedroom and crap everywhere else. Even now, she felt guilt and regret. "Okay, I hear you. Maybe I do like Jess. She is pretty fascinating, after all. And maybe I did push the competitiveness a little too far—"

Jamie raised her eyebrows. "A little?"

"All right, I pushed it way too far. But that doesn't necessarily mean anything."

"If you say so, Alex." Jamie patted her lightly on the knee. "If you say so."

Long after Jamie had left, Alex couldn't quite shake her words. She was right. Of course, she could be competitive, especially when she found herself attracted to someone. She wasn't exactly sure why—she'd always been that way. And as Jamie had reminded her, she had a tendency to take it too far. Becky sure was evidence of that. She could still hear Becky's words ringing out just before she left. *I may love you, Alex, but I can't be with someone I always have to compete with. Love shouldn't be a competition.* A condemnation of her incessant need to win.

So, why had she nearly killed herself trying to keep up with Jess? Yes, she was fascinating. Yes, she wouldn't mind being her friend. But was there more to it as Jamie had suggested? The more she thought about the race and her need to push on at all costs, she had to admit that there might be a bit more to it after all.

* * *

On Sunday Jess rolled through the front door of her parents' house. Her arms and pecs were killing her. Not really surprising. When she had crawled out of bed, every muscle in her chest and arms screaming in agony, she had been forced to concede that she might, *just might*, have gone too hard. Her time had been a personal best so all in all it was worth it.

"Jessiebess!" When she entered the kitchen, her sister, Jordan, cried out, leaped off the barstool, ran over, kneeled down and wrapped her arms around her. "How's my big sis?" Although only ten months separated them in age, Jordan never wasted an opportunity to point out that she was younger.

"Hey Jordan. I'm fine; and you?" Jess leaned over and returned her hug.

Jordan stood and tucked her loose bangs back over her right ear. Although there was no denying that they were sisters—they were sometimes mistaken for twins—Jordan's long shoulder-length brunette curls were a stark contrast to Jess's short pixie cut. "You know me. I'm always good."

Jess chuckled. Jordan was always the same. She wasn't just a glass half-full optimist—she was a glass completely full and pouring over optimist. Maybe it was how their parents raised them but she also tried to find the best in everything. It was hard not to be bitter, angry, not to cry out, why me? Everyone facing a major life-changing disability had to wrestle with those feelings. She faced them every day. But she would hear her mom and dad saying, "Just find the good in the situation." Their family motto. And more than anything, it had probably helped pull her through the dark days after the accident.

Jordan's husband Tim walked over and clapped her on the back. "So how did the big track star do in her race yesterday?" Married to her sister for nearly eight years, Tim was more of a brother than a brother-in-law. At five foot ten, he was within an inch of Jordan's height. The practicality of him being an attorney tempered perfectly Jordan's head-in-the-clouds artist personality. Even his prematurely-graying black hair enhanced his perpetual levelheadedness.

"I didn't do too bad but boy am I feeling it today." Jess laughed and rubbed her left arm with her right hand.

"That's my sis, always pushing herself too far. What was it this time? Couldn't bear the thought of coming in second?"

Her sister knew her well but this time it had more to do with proving herself in front of someone instead of merely winning a race. "I was racing with someone and I guess I overdid it a bit." It was mostly true.

Jordan pulled up a chair. "Oh, you found someone to *race* with you? About time." She gave Alex a devious wink. Leave it to Jordan to try to make something innocent into something lascivious.

"It's nothing like that, Jordan." Jess felt her cheeks burn.

"Too bad. Who was it anyway?"

For some reason, her face grew warmer with each second. "It was that doctor I told you about. Alex."

"What, the *bitch*?"

"Jordan! *Language!*" Their mother Linda called out from across the kitchen where she was preparing lunch with their father Pete.

"Sorry, Mom." Jordan lowered her head and cringed, looking completely sheepish.

Tim rolled his eyes and shook his head at his wife.

"That's the one." Jess laughed, her aching sides made even sorer. She couldn't keep anything from her sister. Other than Terra, Jordan was her greatest confidant, so she had heard the entire sordid story the moment she got home. Jordan's response had mirrored that of Jess and Terra—what a bitch.

"What was she doing there? Come to insult even more disabled folk?"

"No, it was nothing like that. She wanted to make up for what she said. So she ran with me."

"I would've loved to have seen that—her trying to keep up with my sister, the speed demon."

Jess always loved hearing the pride in Jordan's voice when she spoke of her. "I did have to slow down toward the end. I swear, I thought she was going to keel over at one point but she did really well."

"Too bad you didn't finish her off. Would have served her right."

"Actually, Alex isn't that bad. She was a lot of fun to run with and she was even a good sport when she looked as if she might collapse." Jess smiled, picturing Alex on the ground just past the finish line.

Jordan suddenly gasped, covering her mouth. "Oh my God, Jess, you *like* her."

"What? Me like her?" She tried to shrug it off nonchalantly.

"You do! I can see it all over your face." Jordan stared at her in that knowing way that only sisters could.

"She's okay, that's all." Jess wasn't about to admit anything more, especially to Jordan. She would never hear the end of it.

"You sure know how to pick 'em, Jess. Take the most confrontational, combative, hotheaded, competitive, arrogant—" she lowered her voice so their mom wouldn't overhear "—*bitch* imaginable and that's the one you go for."

Tim watched them, his eyes darting from one to the other, while shaking his head. "I'll never understand women. Why would anyone want to be around someone like that?"

Jordan snorted. "Oh please, hon, who are you trying to kid? You're a lawyer—confrontational, combative, hotheaded, competitive and arrogant are just part of the job qualifications."

At Tim's dumbfounded look, Jess burst out laughing again with Jordan. Tim was the kindest lawyer on the planet. Probably why he worked mostly in family law, specializing in adoptions.

With the table set, Pete and Linda called the family together. Jess and Jordan owed their good looks to Linda, sharing the same small, heart-shaped face and dark brunette hair color, with the beginnings of silver streaks that had cropped up over the past few years. Pete, on the other hand, looked nothing like his daughters being a big barrel-chested bear of a man. He and Jess shared the same deep brown eyes, those endless pools of darkness.

After quickly saying grace, they all dove in. This was one of Jess's favorite meals—grilled chicken bruschetta with homemade garlic bread and red wine. She had inherited her mom's love of all things Italian.

After a few minutes, Linda dabbed her lips with a linen napkin. "Sounds like you had fun yesterday, Jess."

Jess quickly gulped down her mouthful. "Yeah, it was actually a blast even though I overreached." She massaged her tender arm.

"I wish you'd let us come watch sometime."

Jess fought back a groan. This was a very old argument. Of course, her parents being who they were, wanted to support her in every way. They had always been that way and even more so after her accident. She appreciated it—she really did—but they

were involved in so many aspects of her life since the accident, she also needed something, anything, no matter how small that she could call entirely hers. Competitions were just that. She could win or fail all on her own, without her parents or Jordan there as a safety net. She needed this bit of independence. "I know, Mom—"

Jordan broke in. "Come on, Mom, you know this is something Jess wants to do by herself. She needs something of her own. We all do."

If Jordan weren't so far away, she'd throw her arms around her. From across the table, she mouthed a silent thank-you.

"I know, Jordan." Linda took a deep breath. "But you can't blame a mother for wanting to cheer on her child. Jess knows that."

Jess also took a deep breath that mirrored her mother's so completely it would have been comical under different circumstances. "I do, Mom, and someday maybe..."

"That's all I ask."

Later, Jordan walked Jess out to her car. Before Jess climbed in, Jordan kneeled down and leaned in close. "Hey, don't worry about Mom, okay? You and I both know she can be a little...a little..."

"Overbearing?" Jess laughed.

"Wasn't going to put it *quite* that way but yeah. But she also means well. She just worries about you, about anything happening. She wants to always be there to help."

Jess had to force herself not to grind her teeth. "I know that but for God's sake I'm not helpless."

"I know that and you know that and deep down, Mom even knows that. The problem is the two of you are just alike—obstinate to the bone. You're as stubbornly independent as she is stubbornly protective."

"Gee, thanks, Jordan. And what about you?"

"Me? I'm the sweet lovable one."

Jess suddenly snorted out a laugh loud enough to scare several birds from the feeder. She reached out and lightly

punched her sister in the arm. "If that's not the biggest load I've ever heard…"

Jordan smiled and put on her best ain't-I-so-innocent look.

Jess slid in behind the wheel, folded up her chair and tossed it behind her. Jordan stood up and leaned in through the window, planting a kiss on Jess's cheek. "See you later, sis."

"Later Jordan."

As she backed down the driveway, Jordan cupped her hand to her mouth and yelled. "Hey, don't overdo it with that doctor you have the hots for."

All Jess could do was shake her head as she drove off. Sometimes Jordan was too much but she loved her anyway. Actually, she couldn't ask for a better sister. She could read her like a book.

Once home, she wheeled into her living room. Her arms and chest still ached but nowhere near as badly as earlier. Could Jordan possibly be right? Had she simply been trying to impress the doctor? Alex *was* beautiful. Even when she had been pissed at her, she had noticed how attractive she had been with her jaw-length dirty blond hair and toned, athletic body. She would've had to have been blind not to notice that. And what about the tension between them? Was it merely an adversarial relationship with a healthy dose of competition topped off with a hint of attraction? Was there more to it than that? Did she have the hots for Alex? She wasn't ready to admit that but she couldn't deny that there was *something* there. Whatever was going on, she should still call Alex and see how she was doing today. If she felt this sore, she couldn't imagine how she was feeling.

* * *

As her cell rang, Alex slowly turned her head toward the sound. It was about all she could manage. Sure enough, it sat on the couch beside her, just out of reach. "Damn." She leaned over, trying her best to slide her arm out, but instead of being able to reach her phone, she slumped over on her side, lifting her phone to her ear. The wafer thin piece of aluminum and glass technology felt more like a brick in her hand.

"Hey." That was about the extent of her energy.

"Hey, Legs, this is Jess."

"Jess!" Alex sprang bolt upright. "To what do I owe the pleasure?"

Jess laughed, a soft, relaxed sound. "I was just calling to see how you were doing today. Did you survive?"

Alex joined in laughing, feeling as if she were back in her sorority, surrounded by her sisters during a late-night gossip session. "I'm a little sore today. Nothing too bad." An all-time understatement. "How about you?"

"Yeah, I'm a bit sore too. Nothing serious. I'm surprised you're not totally wrecked today. You really pushed it yesterday."

"Actually…" Alex bit her lower lip. She had might as well come clean. "Truth be told…I can barely move." Her voice rose as she finished, a distinct whine creeping in, but she figured she was entitled.

Jess burst out laughing. "Oh, so the truth comes out. I was wondering. How bad is it?"

"I'm not kidding, Jess. I don't think I've ever felt this sore. Every muscle in my body hurts. I can't lift my arms, I can't lift my legs, even my hair hurts."

"Sounds like you really *did* overdo it." There was a definite lightness to Jess's voice. She seemed to be quite enjoying this. "What I find that helps when I overdo things is a nice long bath—as hot as you can stand it."

Thinking about Jess at the same time as a nice hot bath sent a shiver up her spine. She wasn't exactly sure which was more exciting, Jess or the bath or better yet, both together. She hurt way too much to give it much consideration at the moment. Finally she swallowed. "Um…I might give that a try then."

"You do that. I guarantee you'll feel better. Give me a call tomorrow and let me know how it went."

"Will do."

"Oh, and Legs…" Jess lowered her voice. "I had a great time yesterday."

"Me too, Wheels. Me too."

After she hung up, Alex stared at the phone in her hand. Jess had been the last person she had expected to call. And

out of concern too. Apparently they were beyond her socially-insensitive faux pas, thank God. Again, she thought of Jess and that shiver ran up her spine, a feeling she hadn't felt in a long time. But did it mean anything? The more she thought about it, the more she decided that she might, just might, like to find out. She was going to follow Jess's advice and throw herself into a hot bath. What could be better than that? Alex laughed. The only thing better would be a nice hot bath for two.

CHAPTER FOUR

On Monday at seven in the evening Alex walked through the ER to begin her shift. Although she was still a bit sore and stiff, she felt worlds better. Jess had been right—the bath had been just the ticket. Actually, it had been so relaxing that she had fallen asleep and had woken up an hour later pruned in cold water. She smiled at the thought.

"Hey Doc, you seem to be in high spirits today. Have a good weekend?" Maria, her favorite charge nurse, called out as she bounded around the corner. In her mid-fifties, Maria had more energy than half the nurses half her age. In fact, with her still-black hair and barely a line on her face, she looked more like someone in her late thirties.

"Actually, I *did* have a good weekend."

"It shows." Maria threw a hand on her hip, giving Alex the once-over. "I don't think I've seen you this happy in I don't know when."

Alex opened her mouth in denial, but froze. Maria had a point—she *was* happier than any time recently that she could

remember. Had she really been that down? Maybe she had. She certainly felt burned out. But that didn't seem as bad today. Finally, she just smiled. "Why thank you, Maria." What else could she say?

"So, what's up? Some hot date? New girlfriend?"

If it were anyone else, it would feel like prying—everyone knew what a private person she was—but with Maria it was different—she genuinely cared. Alex was immensely appreciative. Sometimes being a doctor was lonely. "Actually, it wasn't a date. I ran a 5K on Saturday with a woman I met through Jamie's professional lesbians of West Michigan group."

"You ran a 5K on Saturday?" Maria stared at her, mouth agape. "You're going to put us all to shame, Doc. The only way you could get me to run a 5K is if there was a double chocolate fudge cake with chocolate frosting waiting at the finish line."

Alex had to laugh. Maria's obsession with chocolate was legendary in the ER. Yet somehow Maria was still rail thin. If she didn't exercise as much as she did and indulged in chocolate as much as Maria, her waistline would be quite different. The thought of that made her groan. "Don't be too impressed, Maria. I paid for it on Sunday. I could barely move. Even now, I'm still sore and tender."

"Well, you certainly don't look it." Maria eyed her up and down again. "Just thinking about running makes me sore and tender."

"I love it." At least she did. Yesterday while she lay on the couch, every muscle in her body cussing at her, she had her doubts. But today she was warming to the idea again. "I know it's probably hard to believe but that was actually the first time I've ever run with someone. Running has always been a very private thing with me."

"Really? She must be something special. I know what a social butterfly you are." Maria gave her a wink. It was an inside joke between them. Alex was as legendary about her privacy as Maria was with her chocolate obsession.

Alex could feel her cheeks turning a bright pink. Jess was special, there was no denying that. But anything more than that,

she wasn't sure. They were friendly—at least now. They were possibly on their way to being friends—and hopefully very good friends—but anything more... "She is really something, Maria. I don't think I've ever met anyone as focused and driven. You would never believe that she was in a wheelchair."

"Oh." With her lips in the shape of an O, Maria's surprise was comical. "When you said 'running' I was thinking of *running* running, not...I'm not sure what you'd say..." She shook her head. "You know what I mean..."

Alex laughed and clapped her hand to Maria's shoulder. "Don't worry about it. I'm not sure there *is* any proper way of saying it." At least she didn't think there was a proper way to talk about it. Maybe she would have to ask Jess. She certainly didn't want to offend her somehow inadvertently again.

"I guess you're right." Maria simply shrugged. "If you don't mind me asking, how did she end up in a wheelchair?"

Maria's question left her completely stumped. How *did* Jess end up in a wheelchair? That probably should have been one of the first things she asked her. She asked patients those questions all the time. As a friend, it was different—very different. Jess wasn't her patient and it wasn't a professional query. However, Jess probably got that all the time and if it were her, after a while it would become a bit of a sore spot. She didn't want to be like that. If Jess wanted to tell her, she'd tell her. If not, then it really wasn't any of her business. "You know, Maria, I'm not really sure. I didn't want to pry."

Maria waved it off. "Oh well, no big deal right? I'm sure she'll tell you when the time is right."

But it was a *huge* deal. It was Jess's life. And if their first meeting had taught her anything, she should never think of anything concerning Jess as no big deal. Maria was correct though—Jess would tell her when the time was right and from what she had seen of Jess so far, it wouldn't be a second sooner.

Just then, one of the new nurses, MacKenzie, rounded the corner. "Just to give you a heads-up, Dr. Hartway, that drug seeker's back."

Alex rolled her eyes, a smile still firmly on her lips. "Well, I'd better go take care of that."

Maria looked nearly as stunned as when she had told her that she had run a 5K. "You really *are* in a good mood."

As she turned away, the smile even wider on her lips, Alex had to agree with Maria completely. She really *was* in a good mood and even the most annoying, narcotic-seeking repeat patient couldn't change that, not today.

* * *

"Jess, wait up."

Jess was just about to head out the door as Terra ran up. "Hey stranger, haven't seen you all day."

Terra rolled her eyes and let out a long sigh. "I've been in meetings all day. Mom and Dad are brainstorming ways to expand."

"Oh, *that* sounds like fun. So sorry I missed it."

Terra flashed her a snarky glare. "No need to be *that* sarcastic. Next time I'll make sure you're included."

"Ah…yeah, no thanks. I'm fine right where I am."

Terra rubbed the back of her neck. "At least it's over. I don't think I could have looked at another pie chart without losing it. I'm absolutely brain dead. I don't mind planning meetings but not *all* day."

Jess could understand. The equivalent of managerial waterboarding. She needed to move around. Sometimes even running the Espresso Book Machine could be a bit much for her. "I hear you. Why don't you come work out with me at the club?"

"Yeah right. You might as well just shoot me now."

"It might help you work off some stress."

"I've got my own ways of working off stress. A horror film and a big bottle wine."

Jess laughed and shook her head. "To each their own I guess."

"Ain't that the truth." Terra high-fived Jess. "I wanted to catch you before you left—I haven't talked to you since Saturday. How are you doing?"

"Still a bit sore." Jess rubbed her arms.

"I'm not surprised. You looked half-dead at the finish line and I thought the good doctor had had a heart attack. What was up with that?"

Jess shrugged. "Just a little friendly competition."

"Friendly competition my butt. The two of you looked as if you were out to run each other into the ground."

"Okay, I admit there *may* have been a bit of pent-up resentment on my part. I don't know about Alex—she just seemed to have something to prove."

"Maybe that she isn't a total ass."

"Trust me, Alex isn't like that. She made a mistake and she owned up to it. You've got admire that."

"If you say so."

Jess had to smile. Hell hath no fury like Terra when one of her friends is scorned. No matter what, Terra seemed determined not to like Alex. It was great to have such a good friend. She had no doubt that if need be, Terra could really tear into someone, which was so ironic since she was usually so quiet and mild-mannered. "Alex is really pretty sweet. You should have heard her yesterday."

Terra's eyes flew wide open. "You talked to her yesterday too?"

"I called to see how she was doing." Jess chuckled as she remembered Alex's agonized voice. "She could hardly move. She sounded so miserable. It was actually pretty cute."

Terra looked at her more closely, her eyebrows knitting together. "Cute, huh?"

"Oh yeah. I think I may have pushed her a little too hard. She couldn't lift her arms or legs so I told her to go take a long hot bath."

"Oh no, don't tell me. You *like* her." Terra slumped against the new release shelf.

"What?" First Jordan and now Terra. What was she giving off, some strange *I like Alex* vibe? Did someone pin a sign to the back of her chair? "I'm sure I don't know what you mean."

"Oh yeah, I can see it in the moony way you get when you talk about her." Terra shook her head in disbelief.

If Terra hadn't looked so adorable with her utter hangdog look, Jess might've been a bit miffed. But for all of Terra's bluster, she knew she meant well. "Well, if that *is* the case—and I'm not saying that it is—but *if* it is, you're going to have to start being nice to her."

"Ah…ah…ah…" Terra stared at her, her mouth dropping open. It was easy to see that she was hard at work running the concept through her head.

"Something to think about." With a laugh, Jess wheeled out the door, calling back over her shoulder as she went. "See you tomorrow."

Since she always worked out on Mondays, Jess drove across town to her favorite gym, East Town Fitness Center. It helped that she knew the owners too, Mike and Bev. Before her accident, she had been a regular. Then when she was recovering, Mike and Bev had gone out of their way to help her with her rehabilitation. They became like her surrogate parents and the staff were like her adoptive family.

Twenty minutes later, she rolled through the front door. Mindy, one of the newest fitness trainers, looked up as she entered. Tall, tan and muscular, Mindy would not have looked out of place on the cover of a fitness magazine. In fact, any time Jess saw her, the song by the Commodores, "Brick House," began playing in her head. "Hey Jess, good to see you girl."

"Hi Mindy." Jess glanced around. "Looks like it's pretty slow in here today."

"It's been like that all day. You sure know how to pick the best time."

It wasn't an accident at all that she knew the best times to go to the gym when there would be the fewest people there. Over the years, she had found late Monday afternoons tended to have the fewest. Probably because everyone was busy recovering from the weekend and trying to get back into the work week. Whatever the reason, she preferred not to work out in front of a gawking crowd. "Well if you're not busy, Mindy, could I get you to spot me?"

"Sure thing girl." With a big smile, Mindy clapped her on the shoulder and followed her across the gym to the bench press.

Jess slid out of her chair and lay back on the bench, scooting into position underneath the bar. Mindy helped line her up and spotted her as she took the bar. Her muscles were still pretty tender, especially her shoulders and pecs, but she wasn't going to let that stop her. No pain, no gain and all that. But just as she was about to do her last rep, her muscles gave out and thankfully Mindy caught the bar and heaved it back into the cradles.

"Whoa girl, almost got you there. You okay?"

Jess pushed herself up into a sitting position, breathing hard. "I'm fine. My arms just gave out at the end there. I'm still recovering from Saturday."

Mindy threw her a towel. "Oh, and what was it this time? West Michigan triathlon? Great Lakes Iron Woman competition? Extreme downhill mountain hand cycling?"

Jess flicked Mindy with the towel. As much as she would like to deny it, she did have a reputation around the gym for pushing herself to the limit in some of the most grueling local competitions. "No, it was nothing like that. I just did a benefit 5K."

"Really and you're still recovering? A 5K for you is like a walk in the park." Mindy sat down on the bench beside her.

"Well…" There was no use lying about it so she might as well come clean. "I *may* have overdone it a bit."

"*You?* Overdo it a bit? I can't imagine you would do that, not Jess the cautious and careful." Mindy's voice dripped with sarcasm.

Okay, she deserved that. This certainly wasn't the first time she had been in this state. She had always been driven, even before her accident. And after that, she had become more so. It probably contributed to the speed of her recovery. "Yeah, yeah. I know what you're going to say."

"Well, you're going to hear it again." Mindy fixed her with a stare that would have sent even the most unruly child begging for mercy and forgiveness. "I say this not only as a professional

trainer but also as a friend. You really need to watch how much you push yourself. It's great that you do so many activities and work so hard but you also need to have some common sense. As much as you don't want to acknowledge it, you *do* have limitations."

Jess shot her a deep scowl.

Mindy smiled, her look softening. "Scowl all you want but you have to realize that your arms do double duty—not only are they your arms but they're also your legs. So when you overdo it, say in a 5K race, that also affects your ability to lift, to pick things up, to do any of those thousand little tasks each day that requires your arms."

Jess couldn't ignore Mindy's admonishment. And it wasn't as if she hadn't heard it all before.

"What made you push yourself so hard anyway?"

At the question, Jess felt her cheeks grow warm. "Well…you see…there was this woman—"

Mindy burst out laughing. "Forget I asked. Now it all makes sense."

Her cheeks were now blazing hot. What could she say? She had gone overboard because of Alex. Seemed like everyone had come to that conclusion—her sister, Terra and now Mindy. She could tell herself all she wanted that she had done it to teach Alex a lesson but deep down she knew that wasn't entirely the case. It may have begun that way, but seeing Alex's determination and drive had changed it. Not to mention that the woman was striking, especially in her running shorts and a tank top.

"So, who was this woman? Some hot new girlfriend?" Mindy squatted beside Jess and nudged her in the ribs with her elbow.

Her face felt as if it were three degrees shy of the sun's surface. "No, no, nothing like that." But as she said it, somewhere inside her head, a little voice finished with, *not yet*.

Jess's stomach tightened, sending a quick jab of pain through her abs. *Not yet? Not yet what?* Where had that come from? Of course she found Alex attractive. And sure, she was intriguing. But think of her as anything more than a possible friend? That would just be absurd.

Mindy laughed at her startled expression. "Too bad. There's nothing like a good romance to justify overdoing it."

"Yeah, I guess you're right." She didn't know what else to say. Since her accident, she had never really entertained the possibility of romance. Sure, a lot of people with spinal injuries had deeply-fulfilling romantic lives, some with injuries much more severe than hers. But for her, romance just wasn't an option. If she were to be in an intimate relationship, it would have to be on equal terms. Losing the use of her legs pretty much prevented that. If she wasn't able to give one hundred percent then it wouldn't be fair to either her or someone else.

"So, what you say we go work on some stretches—try to get your arms back in shape."

Her heart really wasn't into the workout anymore. Forty minutes later as she left the gym, she still couldn't shake the notion that there might be a little more to her feelings toward Alex. Anything more than friendship wouldn't be fair to either of them. But there was nothing preventing her from forming a close friendship with Alex—nothing at all.

She pulled out her cell and hit Alex's number. The phone immediately went to voice mail and she hung up. "Damn." She quickly punched in a text.

* * *

Alex settled down for a much-deserved break just after midnight. What a crazy night it had been so far. She had stitched up no less than five different hands—apparently tonight was the night for people to stick their hands where they shouldn't be. She had fished out foreign objects from two different kids—a small Lego minifigure hammer from the nose of a sweet little three-year-old boy and a small red Lego flower from the ear of his equally adorable twin sister. Apparently the two had made up their own game to hide things much to their distraught parents' horror. Twenty minutes later, the kids were fine. It had actually been harder on Mom and Dad.

But the real highlight of the night had been when twenty-three people, all from the same family, came in with a wicked case of food poisoning. Great-aunt Martha had made her famous secret recipe spinach dip for Grandmama's ninetieth birthday party. Turns out the secret ingredient for her secret recipe was five year out-of-date mayonnaise. So many people in one place chucking and running to the bathroom. This had been on top of all the usual bumps, bruises, breaks, colds, flu and general craziness that breezed through the door of the ER on any given night. Not that she gave much credence to it, but at one point she checked if it were by chance a full moon—anything to explain the madness.

She closed her eyes for a moment, doing her best to relax, before she opened her Greek yogurt and small baggie of grapes. That and her açaí juice made up her lunch, a much healthier alternative than most of her co-workers favored. And being after midnight, the cafeteria was closed, not that she would chance that unless she was desperate and had no choice. She pulled out her cell phone to check her messages—hospital policy prevented her from leaving it on. A text message popped up from Jess. *Hey, just seeing how you're doing. Call me when you get this, anytime night or day.*

Alex glanced up at the clock on the wall. Twelve twenty-five—it wasn't that late, was it? It *was* anytime day or night, and after the wild night she had so far, she could certainly use the distraction. Taking a deep breath and holding it, she quickly punched in Jess's number. One ring…two rings—was this a good idea? Three rings…four rings—still no answer. Just as she is about to hang up, the line picked up.

"Hello." Jess drew out the word, her voice heavy with sleep.

Alex winced. What had she been thinking? Who called someone at this hour? She should've known better but it was too late now. "Hey Jess, it's me. Sorry to be calling so late."

"Legs?" Jess's voice perked up on the other end.

"Yeah, it's me. Again, I'm sorry it's so late but you said call anytime and—"

"No, no. It's fine." Jess laughed softly. "I'm glad you called. I wanted to see how you were doing. Yesterday you sounded pretty rough."

Alex leaned back in her chair. "Actually, I'm doing a lot better." She flexed her legs. Now only a dull ache instead of intense agony. "Your suggestion of a bath really did the trick."

"Good, I'm glad. Nothing beats it for muscle aches and pains."

"You're absolutely right." Alex smiled to herself. Again the thought popped into her head—nothing except maybe a hot bath for two.

Jess was quiet on the other end, her breathing slow and deep. Alex listened. Still nothing. Did they get disconnected? Did Jess fall asleep? The moment drew out. Finally, she cleared her throat. "Jess, you still there?"

"Yep, yep. Sorry about that." She laughed. "I think I dozed off there a second."

"I can let you go."

"No, that's okay. I'm glad you called. So what are you doing so late?"

"Actually I'm at work. I usually work the late shift in the ER." She popped another grape into her mouth.

"I didn't know that."

"Usually unless I take a double shift. That's what I'd done just before I showed up at the restaurant when I made…well… um…"

"Made an ass of yourself?"

"Yeah, when I made an ass of myself. Talk about making a first impression."

"You certainly made an impression, I'll give you that." Jess again laughed softly, not a trace of bitterness at all.

"I should have just gone straight home instead." Alex had to smile to herself. At least Jess could joke about it now.

"I for one am glad you didn't or I may have never had a chance to meet you, Legs."

"I'm glad too."

"Well in that case, how about we get together later this week if you're not too busy?"

Alex snapped up straight. Jess wanting to get together—that was the last thing she would've expected but she surely wasn't going to complain. "I would love to. What do you have in mind?"

"There's a 5K run over in Grand Haven."

"Um…" Another 5K? What was Jess trying to do, kill her in the most torturous way possible?

Jess burst out laughing on the other end. "I'm just kidding."

"You just wait. I'll have to get you for that."

"Promises, promises." Jess continued to laugh. "Tell you what—why don't we just plan on Wednesday evening, if you're not working, and come up with something then? I'll text you tomorrow with some thoughts."

"Sounds good to me." On the other end, Alex could hear Jess trying to stifle a yawn. "I should probably let you go back to sleep now."

"Yeah, you're probably right—" Jess yawned again "—I'm glad you called though, Legs."

"Me too. Good night, Wheels."

With the new spring in her step, Alex popped the last two grapes into her mouth, grabbed her drink and nearly skipped out the door. A wide grin plastered her lips. Her coworkers might wonder, but after the conversation she had just had with Jess, she didn't care. Give her colds, flu, dismembered limbs, hell, give her more food poisonings—she felt as if she were ready to take on anything that might come in. Nothing could get her down. With a deep breath, she puffed up her chest and looked toward the entrance. "Bring it on."

CHAPTER FIVE

At quarter to six on Wednesday, Alex pulled up in front of Jess's house in Rockford and looked out the window. It was a nice upscale neighborhood with large mature maple trees lining the street. She'd actually thought about living in Rockford herself before she had decided on East Grand Rapids. Its proximity to the hospital won out.

Alex still had no idea what Jess had planned for the evening. All she had sent in her text was the time, her address and to wear comfortable shoes. She had found Jess's place easily and with fifteen minutes to spare. Better than being late. That was what had gotten her into trouble at their first meeting. Alex laughed to herself. Actually shooting off her mouth had been the problem but being late hadn't helped. As for the comfortable shoes, she only hoped Jess wasn't planning anything too strenuous. She still hadn't fully recovered.

Alex quickly walked up the sidewalk and climbed the long ramp leading up to the porch. She hadn't given it much thought before but even the simple task of entering a house must prove

a challenge to Jess. How many other little things did she have to contend with each day? She smoothed her dark purple cotton V-neck and ran her fingers through her hair before pushing the doorbell. At the chime, she stepped back and waited. Not ten seconds passed before Jess opened the door and waved her in.

"I see you made it."

"Yeah, it wasn't hard to find at all."

"Great and I see you wore comfortable shoes too." Jess nodded toward Alex's favorite Merrell Moab Ventilators.

"Yes." Alex drew out the word with a slight cringe. She still wasn't sure what she was in for. Knowing Jess, it could be anything.

Seeing her apprehension, Jess laughed. "Don't worry, Legs, I'm not going to make you run another race or anything like that."

"Oh, thank God." Alex blew out a sigh of relief. Her poor legs would surely mutiny if she tried that again so soon. "So what *did* you have in mind?"

"One of the reasons I chose this house was the White Pine Trail, so I figured what could be better than a nice leisurely stroll on this beautiful evening." A wide smile with just a hint of mischief lit up Jess's face. "You think you're up for that?"

Alex didn't miss the friendly taunting. "You bet. Just lead the way." As she followed Jess out the door, she felt her competitive streak lying in wait just out of sight. Had Jess suggested running a 5K—or even a 10 or 20K for that matter—she wouldn't have backed down even if it meant crawling the entire distance.

The more she thought about it the more she had to concede that Jamie was right—she had a serious problem with competitiveness. It had served her well growing up. She had won college scholarships, got into medical school and quickly risen to the top during her residency and through the ranks to her current position.

But when it came to interpersonal relationships, her need to win at all costs had laid waste to many bridges, the worst probably being Becky. She had really muffed that one up. Everything was a competition—who could finish brushing their teeth first,

who outdid whom on Valentine's Day, who gave more in their relationship? Even intimacy was a competition. She didn't want to make that mistake again with Jess, even if they were only friends. Still, she had to fight that nearly uncontrollable feeling that rose up from the pit of her stomach and cried out, *go go go!*

"What are you thinking about, Legs?" Jess rolled easily beside her as they headed south over the Rogue River bridge on the trail. People were out walking in both directions, enjoying the balmy late June evening. "You're a million miles away."

"Sorry about that." Alex broke her reverie. She could deal with her competition obsession later. For now, she should just enjoy the beautiful evening and Jess's company. "It's just so nice out, you caught me daydreaming." She laughed softly. At least that was half true.

Jess nodded. "I do that a lot too. Almost every night as long as the weather permits, I go out on the trail, most of the time lost in my own thoughts."

"I can certainly see why." Alex looked up and down the trail, which shot off in both directions as straight as an arrow, the remnants of its life as a railroad. The views were breathtaking. In spots, large mature trees lined both sides, their branches closing in over top to form a canopy. In other sections the ground dropped away just beyond the trail, falling sometimes two hundred feet down to the Rogue River.

She glanced at Jess and her breath stuck in her throat. If the scenic trail vistas were breathtaking, it had nothing on Jess as the sunlight streamed down through the branches and illuminated her. Her dark hair glowed and the light glistened off the thin sheen of sweat covering Jess's arms, the top of her chest, up her slender neck and over her small heart-shaped face. A beautiful sight right down to Jess's black leather fingerless gloves. "Do you ever take those gloves off?" She blurted it out before she thought.

"What did you say?" Jess came to a quick stop and wheeled around to face her.

Alex immediately winced and closed her eyes. What on earth had she been thinking? Had she learned nothing when

it came to blurting things out? "I'm sorry...I didn't mean...I should never...none of my..." All she could do was stammer.

Jess chortled. "That's so cute when you do that, stumbling over your words like you do."

Alex opened one eye and peeked over at Jess. She certainly didn't seem upset. But then again, she didn't want to put her foot in her mouth again, even if they were shod in her favorite Merrells. "I didn't mean to pry. It's really none of my business."

"No, no, that's not why I said that." Jess was shaking her head, still laughing. "This time I was the one daydreaming and I seriously didn't hear what you said."

Alex blew out a sigh of relief. Thankfully she was just being paranoid. Still, she didn't want to do anything to upset Jess. "Believe me, it was nothing. It was just a stupid question."

Jess wheeled closer, a look of concern washing over her face. "Alex, don't worry so much. If you have a question, go ahead and ask it. I promise I won't bite. I'd rather people ask questions than for them to make assumptions."

Alex relaxed. As Jess had said, maybe she did worry too much. If she had a question, she should just ask it. "I was just wondering, do you ever take those gloves off for anything?"

Jess held up her right hand and flexed her naked fingers, the black leather taut over her hand. "Nope, I never take my gloves off for any reason." She laughed again. "Well, except maybe to put on new ones. I go through at least a pair of month. You should see, I have a whole drawer full of them at home."

"Really? I would have thought they would get uncomfortable after a while."

Jess pointed down at Alex's feet. "Are those shoes comfortable for walking up this trail?"

"Of course, these are the most comfortable shoes I have."

"More comfortable than going barefoot?"

"Well yeah. I couldn't imagine walking up this pavement barefoot. My feet would be nothing but blisters."

Jess held up her hand palm out, showing the thick gel padding. "Same here."

"Oh, now I get it." Alex stood there with her mouth hanging open. She hadn't thought about it that way before. She wore

shoes on her feet—Jess wore gloves on her hand for the same reason. Finally, Alex heaved a big sigh. "I guess there's a lot of things I've never really considered before. You must think I'm a total idiot."

"No, I don't think that at all." Jess smiled and motioned to a bench set alongside the trail. "Why don't we have a seat?" She waited for Alex to sit while she edged up alongside in her chair.

Alex tucked in, chewing her lower lip. Why she was so nervous around Jess, she didn't know. Most of it had to do with being afraid she would say the wrong thing.

Jess reached out and lightly patted her on the shoulder. "Look Alex, you don't have to be so nervous around me. There's nothing to be afraid of. I'm not contagious or a fragile china doll."

"I know that." Alex turned to look Jess directly in the eyes. "I don't want to look at you like a patient and I don't want you to look at me like your doctor. So that leaves me fumbling around a bit when it comes to what to ask and what not to ask."

"As long as you treat me with respect, there's nothing to worry about. Now by all means, if you have questions, ask them."

"Okay, I'll try." Alex nodded. There was one question she was dying to ask. "How did you…I mean to say…"

"How did I end up in the chair?" Jess lifted her eyebrows.

"Well…yeah. I know it's a very personal question, probably also a very painful one, but I *was* wondering."

"It's not a big deal actually." Jess waved her off. "It happened ten years ago when I was a senior in high school…"

Alex leaned in. The only sound she heard was Jess's voice. She barely noticed the others sharing the trail on foot, on bicycle, with their kids, with their dogs—all she saw was Jess.

"…I was out jogging, trying to clear my head." She let out a soft laugh. "I don't think I've ever told anyone this part before. I was trying to clear my head because just the night before I had realized that I was gay."

"*What?* The day after you realized you were gay?"

"Yep."

"Oh man. That's timing for you."

"Tell me about it." Again the soft laugh. "I had just spent the night with my first girlfriend, Tracy. Before that, I had been really fighting with myself—was I straight or was I gay? That night pretty much answered the question for me. After that there was no denying, I really was gay."

"I think everyone who's gay has had that moment, that epiphany, when there's no denying it any longer."

"Exactly. That was my defining moment. So, here I had all the crap that goes along with that realization spinning around in my head. How was I going to tell my parents, my sister? Would they kick me out of the house? And if they did, where would I go? Then I thought, how was I going to tell my friends? Would they accept me or turn their backs on me? I mean, Grand Rapids sometimes isn't the most tolerant place."

Alex snorted a bitter laugh. "That's one of the things that surprised me the most when I first moved here. Sure, there is a tight lesbian community but the community as a whole can be a little…"

"Puritanical?" Jess lifted her eyebrows.

Alex laughed again. "Good word. I was going to say conservative but puritanical works so much better."

"One of the advantages of working in a bookstore—I'm surrounded by English majors."

Alex leaned back on the bench. She was feeling much more relaxed. A lot of the tension had lifted. Maybe it was just sitting there talking but she figured a big part of it also had to do with Jess's fascinating story.

Jess took a deep breath. "Now where was I? Oh yeah, there I was jogging along with all that whirling around in my head when out of nowhere this truck swerves across the center line and plows into me from behind."

"Oh my God!" Alex clapped her hand over her mouth, stifling the quick gasp.

"I didn't know what hit me. One moment I was jogging along and the next I feel something running into me and throwing me up into the air. I woke up lying in the ditch with some guy sitting beside me."

By now, Alex was sitting right on the edge of the bench. "Then what?" She could barely manage a whisper.

"I knew right away that it was pretty bad. I was numb all over and couldn't feel anything below my waist. I looked down and when I saw the damage, I think I passed out again because the next thing I remember I was somehow propped up with that guy still sitting beside me. At first, I thought maybe I was dead and this scruffy guy was some crazy angel—you know like in some cheesy movie or something. But then he cracked open a can of beer and I thought to myself 'that's a strange thing for an angel to do.' He looked over at me and when he saw that I was looking back, he holds out the beer and says as polite as can be, 'You want one?'"

Jess's story was rivetingly horrific. Alex didn't blink.

"The entire scene was surreal, probably because I was in shock. I remember calmly telling him, 'No thank you, I don't drink.' He just nodded like it was no big deal, like we'd been friends for years. He took a big long drink, smacked his lips, looked at me again and said, 'Damn shame, miss. You're busted up real bad. Not sure you're going to make it.' It was then that I remember real panic setting in. There I was, lying in a ditch with a drunk sitting beside me and thinking to myself, 'Oh shit, I'm going to die.'"

Alex drew in a long gasping breath when Jess paused. She hadn't realized she had been holding her breath the entire time.

"I started crying and asked the guy to call nine-one-one. He just took another sip from his beer and as casually as can be, said he couldn't because he didn't have a cell phone. I begged him to go for help but all he would do was sit there and drink his beer, popping open another one when he finished the first. I kept crying and begging for him to go for help but he just kept saying it's a damn shame. I couldn't move on my own even though I tried to lean over and pull myself out of the ditch, grabbing wads of grass and digging my hands into the dirt."

As she listened, Alex didn't realize that she had been crying. Tears ran down her cheeks as she stared at Jess in disbelief.

Jess cleared her throat, her eyes slightly unfocused as she continued. "I had clawed my way up to the side of the road and finally—not sure really how long—someone drove past and stopped. They covered me up with a blanket from their car and called nine-one-one. I kept thinking, 'Please don't let me die, please don't let me die.' It seemed like forever but the next thing I know, there were flashing lights everywhere and people running every which way. I was put on a spinal board, lifted up on a gurney and wheeled to where Aero Med was waiting." Jess laughed again, this time not sounding nearly as bitter. "First and last time I've ever ridden in a helicopter. The only thing I remember was thinking, 'My God, it's loud in here.'"

Alex laughed with her, the light breeze cool against her wet cheeks. "You've got that right. The few times I've ridden along in Aero Med, I couldn't hear anything for hours afterward. It sounds like a hurricane inside that helicopter."

"After that, I spent six months in the hospital. It was all a jumbled time of tests and surgeries, rehab and counseling. I think by the time I was done, I had had something like eleven different surgeries. When that guy hit me with his truck, the front bumper shattered my pelvis and broke my legs in I don't know how many places, besides the other more obvious injuries."

Alex winced. She knew all too well how surgery could take its toll both physically and emotionally. But to have so many surgeries in such a short time, she shuddered. "If you don't mind me asking as a physician, what was your diagnosis and prognosis?"

"No, I don't mind at all. I don't think anyone's ever asked me in quite that way." Jess smiled.

Alex shrugged.

"My official diagnosis is complete paralysis due to an acute spinal cord transection between levels T-ten and L-one."

Alex felt her stomach churn. Jess would be in that chair for the rest of her life. Even with some of the latest treatments, there still was no chance Jess would ever walk again. Finally, all she could manage was, "Oh Jess, I'm so sorry."

Jess reached over with her gloved hand and gently wiped away the tear rolling down Alex's cheek. Their eyes locked and tilting her head to the side, Jess smiled, a soft yet sad smile. "It's okay, there's no need to cry, Legs. I'm fine—really I am. I've come to terms with everything and I've shed all my tears years ago."

Alex quickly tried to swipe away her remaining tears. She wasn't usually so emotional. Professional detachment was part of the job. But Jess's story had really ripped at her heart. This was personal. She took Jess's hand in hers and squeezed. "I can't believe you're not more bitter. I think I'd be angry all the time."

"I try not to let it get to me. If I let it, yeah, I'd be angry, I'd be bitter, but I've got too many things I want to do to let it get me down. Besides, I'm alive. I could have died. You know, glass half-full." Jess smiled brightly.

Alex had to hand it to her—she wasn't sure that she would be that optimistic. She wasn't exactly a forgive and forget type of person. "You know, you're amazing, Jess. I don't think I could be half as strong as you are if that had happened to me."

Jess laughed. "That's just it though—we never really know *how* strong we can be until the time comes *for* us to be strong."

"You may be right but still for me, it would be hard not to be bitter. Whatever happened to that guy who hit you anyway?"

"Got five years in prison, released in just under eighteen months."

Alex's mouth fell open once again. "You have got to be shitting me! Five years, out in eighteen months?"

Jess gave a small nonchalant shrug. "That's pretty much the maximum for operating while intoxicated causing serious injury."

"That's not right at all. He should have gotten a lot more time. You wouldn't believe the patients I get in the ER because of drunk drivers." She was livid. This wasn't fair. None of it was fair. Her chest heaved as she breathed hard. It wasn't until she felt the hand on her arm that she finally started to calm down. Jess was smiling back at her. She stared deep into her dark brown

eyes and instead of finding bitterness and indignant rage—what she was sure her own eyes reflected—all she found was a calm warmth that immediately grabbed her heart. "I'm sorry but it's just not right."

* * *

Jess smiled at Alex's outrage. She really was a different woman than she had thought after their first encounter. Alex was anything but the arrogant, heartless bitch that she had first taken her for. There was a deep and genuine compassion beneath that tough, win-at-all-costs exterior. She would never have expected Alex to cry, let alone at her story. She couldn't remember anyone showing such sorrow as Alex had, except for her immediate family. Then again, she had never shared the intimate details of her accident with anyone before, not Terra, not anyone at the bookstore, no one besides family knew what she had really gone through. But why Alex? Why now? She wasn't exactly sure. The only thing she knew was that for some reason it felt right. She took Alex's hand in hers and squeezed. "There are a lot of things in life that aren't right. But I found if you spend too much time focusing on what's not right, it's easy to lose sight of what is."

Alex stared back open-mouthed. "An athlete *and* a philosopher."

Jess waved her off. "I'm hardly a philosopher." She rolled her eyes. "The most I could say is this chair has given me a different position from which to view life."

"Say what you will but I've learned a lot from knowing you and hearing your story."

"Good." Jess wheeled herself back onto the paved trail facing the way they had come. Maybe it had to do with the way they had started out but for some reason, she was deeply pleased to hear Alex say that. Just a week ago, she would never have believed that she would be sitting and sharing her most personal and painful moments with the same woman who had pissed her off so badly she had to leave a restaurant, but here she was. She

knew all too well that life hardly ever worked out the way she had thought it would. "What do you say to heading on back, maybe getting a bite to eat?"

Alex leaped up as if shot by a spring. "Sounds good to me."

As they made their way back up the trail, deep shadows crawled across the pavement. With the sun beginning to set, there wasn't another person in sight either way. The sound of crickets singing drifted up from the woods on both sides. Although dusk was quickly claiming the evening, the gentle breeze wafted a humid and heady aroma of honeysuckle, damp forest and freshly mown grass. The scent was intoxicating. Jess couldn't remember a better night out along the White Pine Trail. "You know, all this time I've been telling you my story. I think it's only fair if now I get to ask you about yours, Legs."

Alex walked along, slowly bobbing her head. "Fair's fair I guess but there's really not much to tell."

"Okay, how about why did you become a doctor?"

"That one's easy…I liked the challenge. I know a lot of doctors say that they get into medicine because they want to save lives or they want to heal people but for me, it was the challenge of it. Sounds kind of shallow, doesn't it?" Alex's steps grew heavy.

Jess winced. Maybe she shouldn't have asked Alex that. Obviously a sensitive topic. But since she had asked, there was no getting out of it now. "I wouldn't say it sounds shallow. Everyone needs something that drives them. For you, it is the challenge of pushing yourself to succeed and there is no shame in that. Take that 5K on Saturday—I don't think I've ever seen someone push themselves that hard before."

Alex peeked over with a sheepish little grin on her face.

Jess laughed. Alex looked more like a precociously shy young teenager than an accomplished professional.

"I do have a problem with pushing myself too much sometimes. I'm not sure why either. It's like giving up is not an option, ever. I have to win, I have to be the best."

"There's nothing wrong with a healthy competitive drive."

"Oh, ho, ho…" Alex groaned. "I'm not sure healthy is the way to describe it. It's caused me more than a few problems. I've lost some close friends because of it so be warned."

Jess peeked over at Alex as they made their way up the trail. Alex seemed to be a million miles off. There was obviously more to Alex's story than she had let on but who was she to pry? If Alex didn't want to share, she didn't want to share. Jess finally broke the silence. "Well, you don't have to worry about me, Legs. I like someone who will push me, no pun intended."

"No pun intended?" Alex turned to her, her eyebrows knitted together. Her eyes flew wide. "Oh, now I get it. Push you as in *push* you. That's bad, Wheels. That's so bad." She was now laughing.

Jess found herself smiling nearly ear to ear. Alex had used her little nickname again. *Wheels.* She liked that. She had found too many people tiptoed around her condition. She was in a wheelchair, get over it. She didn't need people to talk to her in hushed voices—it's not as if she were on her deathbed. She didn't need everyone to treat her as if she were fragile and might break at any moment—it took being hit by a truck, a big bastard of a four-wheel drive truck at that, to hurt her in the first place. Some would say that made her pretty tough. And for the love of God, don't talk about her in the third person while she was sitting right there. What the hell did they think? Since her legs didn't work, her brain must not work either? All she wanted, all she needed was respect. That was all. Normality. That's why she liked the nickname, Wheels. It made her feel like a real person who just happened to be in a chair and not a chair that just happened to hold a person. Small distinction but it made all the difference. She gave her chair and an extra little push, sending it surging slightly in front of Alex. "You know, I like it when you call me that."

Alex took a couple quick steps to catch up. "What, Wheels?"

"Yeah, I like it."

"I'm glad. I wasn't sure how appropriate it was…" Alex made a weird look on her face, a combination between a wince and a grin. "But then you did call me Legs, so I figured it was only fitting."

"That it is, *Legs*. That it is."

"Why thank you, *Wheels*." Alex gave a half-bow, half-curtsy.

They both dissolved into a fit of wild laughter, sending something—a squirrel, possum, one of the neighborhood cats—scurrying through the underbrush. The shadows along the trail grew longer but up ahead the town lights cast a warm glow over the pavement. Jess slowed her pace. She didn't want their walk together to end, not yet, so she searched for anything to keep the conversation going.

"So, being a doctor, your family must be really proud of you." She immediately realized this had been a huge mistake. Beside her, Alex went completely stiff. "Oh, I'm sorry, I didn't mean…"

Alex quickly waved her off, let out a deep breath and relaxed. She came to a stop in the middle of the trail. "No, don't apologize. It's no big deal, really. My family and I have this understanding—I don't try to see them and they can pretend I don't exist." She let out a bitter laugh.

"Oh Alex." Jess didn't know what else to say. What *could* she say? Nothing that would make it better, so instead she wheeled over closer and reached out, taking Alex's hand in hers.

Alex looked down at her hand held tightly in Jess's gloved hand, and smiled. "Like I said, it's no big deal. My dad's a Baptist preacher, real hellfire and brimstone stuff, so it's no surprise that they didn't take it well when I came out. I was just eighteen, my first year in college…" Here she laughed again. "…a Baptist college in Indiana no less, when I met this girl from Ball State that I fell madly in love with. Being young and naïve, I thought if I told them how happy and in love I was, they'd be okay with it—maybe not happy, but okay. Boy was I wrong."

Jess listened intently. She couldn't imagine. Her family had been wonderful, although she hadn't come out until nearly two years after her accident, which had changed not only her but her entire family. So when she did come out and said that she felt relieved and happy, they had all rallied behind her in support. She liked to think that it would have been the same if she had never been hurt but she would never know. Her family had been

so happy that she was alive that she could have announced that she wanted to take up robbing banks and they would have been supportive. "Did they kick you out or something?"

"Yeah, I wish..." Again the bitter laugh. "Getting kicked out would have been preferable. But oh no, not my family. They weren't going to just kick me out—there would be questions. Couldn't have that. So instead, they packed me up and dragged me off to this residential treatment center in Kentucky—you know, pray away the gay. Told everyone I was still in college."

Jess stared, her mouth wide open. She had heard about stuff like this but it always seemed like a bad joke. Who could do that to their own child? It was hard to believe. "Are you serious?"

"I wish I wasn't. I spent the first few weeks there with no contact with anyone. I'm not even sure how long. I was completely isolated. The only thing I was allowed was a copy of the Bible. Then they started with the laying on of hands and praying, sometimes six, eight, ten hours a day. They actually had me half convinced until one morning the counselor, this creepy old guy, said my problem was I needed to know the touch of a man and as luck would have it, apparently he was that man."

Jess was afraid she would throw up. She gasped out a breathy, "No way."

"Yep. That totally freaked me out and I tried to leave right then but they wouldn't let me go."

"Why wouldn't they let you go? You were eighteen, an adult, they couldn't keep you, could they?"

"Apparently, they could. My parents had forced me to sign a bunch of forms when they took me there. I didn't know what I was signing. I would have put my name on anything I was so confused and scared. One of the forms gave my consent to involuntary confinement and treatment. They could then keep me how they wanted, for as long as they wanted. All legal. Nothing I could do."

Jess shuddered. She could hardly believe that something like that could happen. "Did your family know you could be held against your will?"

Alex laughed bitterly. "Like they'd care. As long as I came back home a good submissive Baptist girl to make a good wife for some man and pop out a bunch of kids, what did they care?"

"How did you get away?"

"That's a good question. I'm actually pretty proud of myself—I MacGyvered the lock on my door with a bread tie and a paperclip then snuck out in the middle of the night. Left with only the clothes I was wearing, a simple gray cotton dress that looked more like a flour sack. I made it into town and called my girlfriend. I couldn't think of anyone else. I told her what had happened and she called her mom and her partner. They had friends in the next town over and within twenty minutes, someone was there to take me in. I felt like someone on the Underground Railroad or being smuggled out of Nazi Germany but I swear, they saved my life."

"What about your family? Did you ever see them again?"

Alex slowly shook her head. "Not since the day they dropped me off. I stayed with my girlfriend and her family until I was able to get back on my feet and into college—a completely different college. There was no way I was going back to the Baptist place. I worked super hard, doing everything I could to get the best grades and win scholarships. I knew if I were to ever be totally free, that was the way."

Jess again squeezed Alex's hand in hers. Suddenly, a lot of things made sense—Alex's near obsession with being the best, her drive and ambition, even why she would rant about people she perceived as lazy or taking advantage. It was more than a miracle that she had gotten as far as she had. Pure determination. Alex simply would not give up, no matter what, and that tenacity was with her even now. It was that teenager who had broken out of some freakish fundamentalist asylum that she saw push herself to her physical limits and beyond while running the 5K. It was that same girl that had collapsed, unable to move, yet triumphant. As her grandma used to say, "that girl's got moxie." If she hadn't been impressed before, she surely was now. "I don't really know what to say, Alex."

Alex looked down into Jess's eyes, her expression softening. "Just knowing that you listened is enough. I'm not sure why I opened up like that. I usually don't tell anyone. No one around here knows anything about my past. Probably why I'm so private. I know it drives Jamie and Sue nuts." She laughed, no longer the bitter sound from only minutes before.

"Thank you for sharing all of that, Alex. I'm really touched that you trusted me."

Alex smiled and gave a single nod.

Jess smiled back, locking her eyes with Alex's. She understood how much it had taken Alex to confide in her. In her own way, Alex had had something happen to her that was just as traumatic as being paralyzed by a truck. Just with Alex, it was more difficult to see the damage. It had taken every bit as much bravery for Alex to overcome what she had gone through as it had for her to recover after her accident. Finally, she blinked. "So, what ever happened to the girlfriend that helped you out?"

"We eventually grew apart. I had focused so much on college that she got pushed to the side, something I still regret. But it all worked out in the end. She met someone and the two of them are still together to this day. I talk to them every once in a while along with her mom and her partner. They're pretty much the closest thing I have to family although it's been a couple years since I've been able to see them."

They stood in the middle of the trail, the sun now almost completely gone. They simply looked into each other's eyes, hand-in-hand. The moment drew out. Finally, the rumbling from Alex's stomach broke the silence. They looked at each other and laughed.

"Sounds like we need to get you something to eat, Legs. I think after this, we deserve beer and delivery pizza."

"Now that is a winning idea, Wheels."

CHAPTER SIX

"So how'd your date go last night?" Jordan jogged alongside Jess through Millennial Park.

Jess nearly swerved off the trail. Her little sister wasn't exactly being subtle. Quickly recovering, she focused on the trail ahead. "I have no idea what you are talking about."

"Oh come on, Jess. You went on a long walk with a certain doctor last night, didn't you?" Jordan stopped, a hand on each hip. She was breathing heavily and her light green tank top was sweat-soaked in a triangle between her breasts.

Jess whirled around in her chair, facing Jordan. "So what if I did?"

"You had pizza and beer afterward, right?"

"Yeah, why?" Jess wasn't liking where this was going. She was beginning to regret telling Jordan anything in the first place.

"Then that was the date." Jordan pointed directly at her and gave a firm nod as if the matter was settled once and for all.

Jess buried her face in her hands. She wasn't just *beginning* to regret telling Jordan about her evening with Alex—she was

definitely regretting it. Why couldn't Jordan just let it go? Why did she have to insist on making it more than what it was? Jess finally looked up and fixed Jordan with her eyes. "For the last time, it wasn't a date."

Jordan stared right back at her. "And what would be so wrong if it was, Jess? It might do you some good. There's nothing wrong with a little romance in your life, believe me."

Jess slammed her fists down against the hand rim on her chair. "I've told you a thousand times, romance isn't for me." If she had known calling Jordan would lead to an inquisition, she would have gone for a run by herself.

"And why not, Jess?"

Jess held her hands out wide. "In case you haven't noticed, I'm sitting in a wheelchair."

"And since when has being in a wheelchair prevented you from doing anything? You are the most amazing person I know. There's nothing that you can't do when you set your mind to it. And romance is no different."

Jess bit her tongue. Jordan just didn't get it. How could she explain it to her? Romance and the chair didn't mix, not for her. It wouldn't be fair, not for her, and certainly not for someone else. Finally, she let out a long, weary breath. "Look, Jordan, romance of any sort is not something I am looking for. Yes, I had a great time with Alex last night. Yes, I think she is a great person. Yes, I can see us being really good friends. That's all I'm looking for."

Jordan finally deflated, letting out a long sigh. "Fine. I just don't want you to miss out on anything, Jess. You're my big sis and I want to see you happy."

"I *am* happy." She sounded a little more defensive than she probably should have so she softened her voice. "Really I am."

Jordan walked over, dropped to one knee and wrapped her arms around Jess's neck. "That's all I ever want. Just do me a favor, don't completely close yourself off to any possibility, okay?"

Jess swallowed, a hard lump in her throat. "Okay, I promise."

She wasn't really sure why she was so adamantly against the thought of a relationship. What would it hurt? Had she been

telling herself for so long that it wasn't for her, that she had closed off any possibility? Or could it be something more? Was she using her chair as a crutch? With that thought, she rolled her eyes. Talk about a bad pun!

After her accident, she had tried to keep things going with Tracy. She wasn't out to her family at the time so that alone made it awkward. And they were only eighteen. She and her family had had a hard enough time dealing with her accident, so how could she expect Tracy, supposedly only a friend, to stay? She couldn't imagine Tracy's stress. While she was recovering and coming to terms with life, Tracy was facing her own turmoil—stress for staying, guilt for wanting to go. Acknowledging her own sexuality. So when it came time for college, Tracy had kissed her goodbye and never looked back. She couldn't blame her. Tracy had her whole life ahead of her, all new exciting possibilities, of course she would want to race on ahead unencumbered. At first, it had hurt her almost as much as being hit by the truck. But as time went on, she began the see more from Tracy's point of view. As hard as it was facing her new life, it was perhaps nearly as hard to face a life of living with someone *with* that new life. She held no hard feelings toward Tracy, yet at the same time it had been a valuable lesson—a relationship with someone trapped in a chair was too difficult.

Jordan jumped up, leaned over and gave Jess another hug. "Hey, how about we jog on back and go for some dinner? My treat."

Glad for the change of subject, Jess nodded vigorously. "Sounds good but what about Tim, you know, your better half?"

Jordan stuck out her tongue, the picture of the perfect spoiled baby sister. "He's working late so you get your wonderful, stupendous—did I mention gorgeous?—sister to yourself."

"Wonderful, stupendous and gorgeous? Sometimes Jordan, you're too much."

"That's why you love me." Jordan flipped her hair back and batted her eyes. "Now let's hurry. I'm starving and you're going to tell me all about your date that wasn't a date with Alex."

Jess groaned loudly and slowly shook her head. Sometimes there was no winning with Jordan.

* * *

"Girls' night in!" Jamie held up a stack of DVDs and a jumbo bag of chips as she sashayed through the door.

Sue followed closely behind, a wine bottle in each hand, rolling her eyes. She shot a quick smile at Alex. Jamie wheeled around with a hand on her hip, the bag of chips jutting out to the side, and they all laughed. It had been far too long since they had had a girls' night in. Between all their hectic and conflicting schedules, it was nearly impossible to find a free night. What had once been once a week, they were now lucky to have every month or two.

Not wasting any time, they made their way to Alex's kitchen to uncork the wine. The first bottle was a Fenn Valley sweet riesling, one of Alex's favorites. She took a glass, toasting her friends, and lifted it to her lips. She let out a low moan as the wine splashed over her tongue. The taste was crisp yet sweet, a perfect accompaniment to the spicy Cajun wings she had whipped up. "We need to do this more often."

"Here, here." Sue held up her glass in agreement.

"Definitely." Jamie mumbled around the Cajun wing she was gnawing.

Most of the time when the three of them got together, it was to support one of Jamie and Sue's causes—save the endangered spotted tree weasel or some such. Alex loved her friends and their manic devotion to all things just and right but sometimes a quiet evening sipping wine, gobbling junk food and watching either the latest rom com or horror flick was just perfect.

Jamie grabbed another wing like a wolverine tearing into a Thanksgiving turkey. She daintily wiped her lips with a napkin, as a prim and proper princess at a ball.

"Only you, Jamie. Only you."

"What?" With a hand to her chest, Jamie tried her best to look innocent, failing miserably. "Can't a girl have a snack?"

"Of course. I'm just afraid if I go for a wing, I'll come back missing fingers. Doesn't Sue ever feed you?"

"Hey, don't get me involved in this." Sue backed away, waving her hands out in front of her.

"Honey, you're always involved." Jamie wrapped her arm around her and kissed her on the cheek, leaving a smudge of spicy Cajun sauce.

Alex watched her two best friends. Although they liked to tease each other and half the time they sounded like two old biddies sitting side-by-side in rocking chairs out on a front porch going at it, they were still the sweetest couple. It was hard not to envy them. Who wouldn't want that?

She thought about Jess and the long walk and talk they had shared the night before. She'd never felt that close to anyone. Whether it was the deeply personal stuff they had shared or the long, intimate walk through the deepening evening, she felt herself growing closer and closer to Jess. But was it a wise idea? They had only just met. She didn't usually let her heart rule. She liked to think things through, weigh all the options and then make a decision. Yet whenever she tried to do just that about Jess, her thoughts all jumbled together until she didn't know what to do.

Just then, Jamie snapped her fingers not more than a few inches in front of her face making her jump. "Wha...what?"

Jamie laughed. "Talk about a million miles away—where were you, girl?"

Sue joined in. "Yeah and I thought I zoned out sometimes."

"And speaking of which, where were you last night? I tried all night to get hold of you."

Alex could feel her face beginning to burn and as much as she would like to blame the Cajun sauce, it had nothing to do with the spice. She *had* noticed Jamie's missed calls this morning. She had been hoping that it wouldn't come up, but she should've known better. It wasn't so much that she didn't want to tell them, as she didn't know *what* to tell them. So, she tried innocent nonchalance. "Nowhere in particular."

Jamie pinned her with her eyes, the look of a tiger about to go for its prey. "Oh come on, Alex, what a load of rubbish. You can't expect me to buy that. Now spill it."

Now she had no choice so with a deep breath, she slowly began. "If you must know, I was out last night with Jess."

Jamie choked. Her eyes began to water and Sue clapped her on the back. When she finally recovered, the excitement on her face was unmistakable. "Alex, that's great. It's about time you got out there and found someone."

Alex moaned, dropping her eyes to the floor.

"Whoa, whoa, whoa." Sue shot a firm look at Jamie. "All Alex said was she was out last night with Jess. Don't go ringing wedding bells yet."

Undeterred, Jamie rounded on Sue, her arms crossed and a how-dare-you expression on her face. "All I was saying is I think it's great that Alex met someone. Call me a hopeless romantic, but anytime two people meet, I think it's something to get excited about." She shot Sue a wicked scowl.

Sue snarled right back at Jamie. "Okay, I get that but there's excitement and then there's *your* excitement. All I'm saying is don't go renting a U-Haul and buying wedding dresses for two before you even hear what Alex wants."

Jamie stuck her tongue out at Sue. "Fine, we'll find out what Alex wants."

Alex had been so caught up in the Jamie and Sue show, she was caught off guard when Jamie turned to her. Usually when the two of them got going, it could turn into a three-act play.

"Tell us, Alex, what's going on with Jess? Are you two hitting it off?" Jamie opened her eyes wider. Behind her, Sue slapped her hand to her head.

It didn't look like she had much choice. Besides, maybe talking it over with Jamie and Sue might help clear her head. It certainly couldn't hurt. "There's not much really to say. Jess and I went out for a long walk and had pizza and beer afterward. That's it. I don't really know what else is going on."

"From what I see, it seems like the two of you are certainly hitting it off, right?" Jamie leaned in, looking as if she were holding her breath.

"I guess. I don't really know." This was proving more difficult than she had thought. Instead of clearing her head, it was making it worse.

Sue leaned forward, concern furrowing her brow. "Are you sure you're okay, Alex? I've never seen you indecisive before. You usually have a direct answer for everything."

Alex let out a deep breath. Leave it to Sue to hit it right on the head. She usually *did* have an answer for everything. So why was she finding it such a challenge to figure out how she felt about Jess? It was a simple enough question. "I think that's probably it right there—I usually *do* have an answer for everything, but with Jess, I can't seem to figure out what's going on in my head. I mean…hell, I don't know *what* I mean. It just feels like a big whirlwind."

Jamie laughed and threw an arm around her shoulder. "Sweetie, that's how it's supposed to be. When you first meet someone, it's supposed to feel like a big whirlwind."

"I guess. But it seems awfully sudden. We just met not even two weeks ago and I can't get her out of my thoughts. One moment I'm floating along and the next minute, it feels as if my chest seizes up. I'm not sure what's going on."

Sue pulled out a chair and sat in it backward, facing Alex. "Do you think this has anything to do with Jess being in a wheelchair?"

Now that the question was out there, it was hard not to wonder. Would she be feeling the same if Jess wasn't in a wheelchair? Was that what was causing her to panic? And if so, why? As much as she didn't want to admit it, Sue might have a point. "That might be part of it. I mean, that does bring up a lot of challenges when one person in a relationship has limitations."

"You might be right but you never know, Jess might be willing to deal with your limitations." Sue shot her a wry grin.

Alex opened her mouth to reply, then froze, trying to wrap her mind around Sue's comment. *Her* limitations? *Jess* willing to deal? Finally she was able to wrap her tongue around her thoughts. "What are you talking about? I don't have limitations."

"Jess *did* literally run you into the ground during that race, right?" Sue smiled at her, a mischievous little twinkle in her eye. "She's a whole lot tougher than I think you're giving her credit for. I don't think the question is if *she* can keep up with *you*, I think the question is if *you* can keep up with *her*."

Sue's words hit with the force of a slap. She hadn't thought about it like that. Jess *had* run her into the ground quite literally as Sue pointed out. It had been her that couldn't move the next day, not Jess. Maybe she wasn't giving Jess the credit she was due.

Jamie chimed in. "Everyone has limitations, Alex. That's what's so great about a relationship—each person can complement the other's limitations with their strengths."

"Okay, I guess you guys are right. Maybe I've been looking at this all wrong. Maybe I need to…" Then it hit her, how foolish she was being. She took a deep breath and went on, her voice filled with irony. "…treat Jess like any other person." And hadn't that been what Jess had been saying all along? Wasn't that why Jess had been so angry with her when she was so rude the first time they met? *She wanted to be treated just like any other person.*

With a wide smirk, Sue clapped her hand on Alex's shoulder. "There's hope for you yet, my friend."

Jamie bumped her shoulder into Alex's. "If you're concerned, just take it slow. There's nothing wrong with that."

Sue clutched at her chest as if she had had a heart attack and pretended as if she were about to fall over. "Oh my God. I never in my life thought I'd ever hear those words out of Jamie's mouth. You'd better heed them, Alex."

Sue's amusing theatrics broke the tension. They had given her a lot to think about. But there'd be time enough for that later—now all she wanted to do was get on with the evening. Alex reached out and threw an arm around both Sue and Jamie, pulling them in close. "Thanks guys, you're the best. Now what do you say we grab some wings before Jamie horks them all down?"

Later that night, Alex lay awake in bed, Jamie and Sue's words running through her head. They had actually been a big help with sorting out her feelings. She was still nervous—stomach-twisting, head-spinning, palms-sweating nervous—but who wouldn't be when thinking about the possibility of a new relationship. And was that what she wanted—a relationship? Would that even be what Jess was seeking? Who knew? But as

Jamie had so uncharacteristically suggested, just take it slowly. She was in no hurry, after all. With that thought, she smiled and drifted off to sleep.

* * *

"Hey, Mario Andretti, watch where you're going?" Terra called out from behind the info desk as Jess went racing by.

Jess grabbed the left hand rim and spun around so fast she nearly rocked up on her rear wheels. "You know what they say, if you can't handle the speed, stay out of the fast lane."

Terra jumped back a step. "Whoa, with all that snark, somebody's in a good mood today."

Jess shrugged. "What's not to feel good about?" She *had* been in an unusually good mood the past couple of days. She had Alex to thank for that. She could have done without her little sister wanting to play matchmaker. She was more than content to be happy with a new friend, especially one that wasn't afraid to push her a bit. She liked someone who would challenge her. Too often, she found that most people took one look at her chair and assumed that she was helpless. That was one thing she never wanted to be—helpless.

"I guess." Terra leaned over with her elbows on the desk. "Simon was telling us downstairs that you were doing wheelies with that big eagle hand puppet on your head for the youngsters in the kids' department earlier. Is that true or was he just blowing smoke up my skirt as usual?"

"I may have been doing something of the sort. Anyway, the kids loved it."

"I'm sure. Here they come to the store to look at books and they end up getting a show."

"Well, it's good for them to see someone like me as just another person. I remember when I was young, I was terrified of anyone in a wheelchair. How's that for ironic?"

Terra nodded her head, sending her dreads flying. "Life has a weird way of working out like that, doesn't it?"

"Ain't that the truth."

"Speaking of a weird way of working out, what's up with you and the doc? I haven't heard anything lately but judging from the way you're racing around here, I would have to think that things are going pretty good."

Jess thought about it for a moment. Last thing she wanted was to get into another conversation like the one she had had with Jordan. But with Terra, she probably didn't have to worry about that. "It's going pretty good, Terra. Alex really is pretty sweet."

Terra scowled.

Jess snickered. Terra had the look of a disapproving mother who had just witnessed her kids eating mashed potatoes with their hands in public. "I know, I know…You still haven't fully forgiven her yet."

Terra leaned back, self-satisfaction radiating from her entire being. "Nope, not yet."

Forgive and forget just wasn't in Terra's vocabulary. Still, Jess loved her for it. "Anyhow, we went out for a long walk on Wednesday and really got to know each other. Trust me, she's not the arrogant, self-absorbed bitch she first seemed. Far from it. She had a pretty rough time growing up so it's no wonder she's the way she is. She had to fight for everything to get to where she's at."

"And you haven't?"

Jess didn't want to betray Alex's confidences. However, she wanted Terra to understand just how much Alex had been through. "We all have our chairs, our prisons that we must overcome. Alex is no different. People look at me and the first thing they see is a chair. But I still have my family and my friends who all love and support me. Alex lost all that when she came out." She hoped that wasn't revealing too much.

Terra stood there, stunned. Like Jess, her parents had been nothing but supportive. "You mean her family completely disowned her?" Her voice was now quiet, almost in awe.

"Yep, when she was eighteen."

"That's bullshit." Terra stood up straight, her voice beginning to rise. "No one should have to go through that. It's not like any of us chose to be who we are. That's just…that's just…that's bullshit, that's what that is."

Jess smiled. Terra was now raging with the same righteous indignation toward Alex's family that she had shown toward Alex when she had been insensitive toward her. If nothing, Terra had a keen sense of social justice and that was what made her so special. "Couldn't have said it better myself."

"You tell her she is always welcome here."

The speed at which Terra had changed her opinion about Alex would have been dizzily shocking had not Jess seen it before. Terra had a bigger protective streak in her than anyone she had ever met. "I'll make sure I tell her that." She hid a wide smile behind her gloved hand.

Terra nodded firmly. "Good."

Twenty minutes later, Jess was racing out the door. She grinned every time she thought of Terra's complete one eighty toward Alex. She wasn't sure why that meant so much to her. What was it really to her if Terra didn't care for Alex? Sure, who wouldn't want all their friends to like each other? But with Alex, it was somehow different. Maybe she wanted everyone to see that the first bad impression really wasn't her. But there was more to it, more that she wasn't able to put her finger on.

Just as she was about to climb into her car, her phone rang. Jordan. Jess let out a groan. On one hand she had Terra who hadn't wanted to warm up to Alex and on the other, she had Jordan who was all gung ho for happily ever after. Both women were taking too much interest. Still, she couldn't avoid her sister forever.

"Hey Jordan, what's up?"

"Hey big sis. I was talking to Mom and Dad and they were saying that it was so great having us all together last Sunday, they'd like to do it again this weekend."

That seemed a bit odd. They got together as a family quite often as it was, at least once a month. Something was fishy. "Really? Mom and Dad said that, did they?"

"Yeah, they did. Maybe this time we could have a barbecue and eat out on the deck."

"That sounds like it could be nice." Jess still wasn't sure what was going on but there was something up. Jordan never sounded that excited about a barbecue on the deck.

"We're thinking around noon on Saturday. Oh, and why don't you invite Alex to come along?"

And there it was. She should've known. Again, she let out a long, low groan. "I don't know, Jordan. Like I told you, Alex is just a friend."

"Oh come on, Jess. We all would like to meet her. What's the harm in that?" Jordan nearly pleaded on the other end. "Plus, if you don't invite her, I'm sure Mom will."

Jess closed her eyes. There was no way out of this, not if Jordan had enlisted their mom for help. If there was one person that was more persistent than Jordan, it was their mother. She didn't have a choice. "Fine, Jordan. I'll talk to Alex but I can't promise that she'll be able to come. She's busy at work and I don't know her schedule."

"Great, I'll tell Mom and Dad. See you Saturday."

Jess had no doubt that Jordan was literally jumping up and down at the moment. "Okay, see you Saturday."

"And don't forget to invite Alex." With a giggle, Jordan hung up.

Jess climbed into her car and dragged her chair in behind her seat. One thing about Jordan's invitation, it gave her an excuse to call Alex. She smiled at the thought. She would take any excuse to call Alex.

* * *

Alex was climbing out of the shower when her cell phone rang. Without grabbing a towel, she ran out the door sopping wet and into her living room where she snagged her phone off the end table. Her luck, she was probably getting called into work. So much for a nice relaxing evening. "Dr. Hartway."

"Hey Legs."

"Wheels, what a pleasant surprise." So much better than the hospital calling. As she stood there, she could feel her pulse quicken.

"I hope I haven't caught you at a bad time."

As Alex stood there dripping, she fought back the huge urge to laugh. "No, not at all."

"Good. I just wanted to see what you're doing."

"Not too much here." Again she fought the urge to laugh. "You caught me coming out of the shower."

"Oh, I'm sorry. I guess I did catch you in a bad time. I can call back—"

"Wheels, it's okay." This time she finally did laugh. "Just a little water on the floor, no big deal."

"Oh my God, talk about timing." Jess giggled on the other end, finally sounding relaxed.

"I guess. I didn't have time to grab a towel."

"So what you're saying is I made you run across your house sopping wet and naked?"

There was no use denying it. "Yep, I'm standing in the middle of my living room as we speak."

Jess roared with laughter. "I bet that's quite the sight. Too bad I'm missing it."

What was Jess saying? Was she flirting or just joking around? What should she do? She couldn't very well ask Jess if she was really wanting to see her naked. How would that go? *Oh Jess, too bad you missed seeing me naked, maybe we can do something to remedy that.* Finally, she decided to play it off as nothing. "I was thinking the same thing. That way you could help me clean up the mess."

"Oh, ho, ho. That might be worth it if I got to watch you mopping up the floor naked."

Her mouth was dry. Just the thought of having Jess there with her while she was naked sent a stirring through her stomach, a stirring that was quickly traveling lower. She sucked in a quick breath doing her best at indifference. "I'll have to remember that. I didn't know you had a thing for naked housecleaning." Alex did her best to sound as if she were joking, all the while trying to ignore the increasing heat deep within her.

Jess laughed again. "I walked right into that one, didn't I?"

"Yes you did, and I may never let you forget it either." The light banter was certainly helping take her mind off her sudden arousal. She couldn't remember the last time she had felt that.

"Fair enough. Tell you what, why don't you go towel off, clean up the floor, slip into something comfy—the order's up to you—then give me a call back."

"Sounds like a plan. Call you back in a few." With that, Alex hung up and stared at the phone in her hand. That had certainly been a different conversation, not that she didn't enjoy it. Far from it. It had just been, well—no other way to put it—it had been pleasantly unexpected. If Jess's joking and innuendo were any indication, then perhaps she was also thinking along the same lines. Maybe, just maybe, there was beginning to be more between them than friendship. And with that thought, a huge dopey smile plastered to her face, Alex skipped across the living room and back up the hall to grab a towel.

* * *

Jess set her phone down beside her and giggled wildly. If anyone had heard her, they'd probably think she were a teenager with her first crush. Something about the entire conversation with Alex made her feel silly. Maybe it was being caught off guard and realizing Alex was naked on the other end of the phone. If she were being honest with herself, she found the image exciting, at least mentally and emotionally.

As for physically, she wasn't sure. Since her accident, she hadn't given much thought to physical excitement. That was before—this was after. But as she sat there, she could feel a fluttering of something deep within her, coming from somewhere in her stomach and below. It was a feeling that she hadn't felt in a long time, not in over ten years, not since her accident. Yet at the same time, a subtle tingle raced up her body, over her breasts, her arms, her neck and across her face. But what did it mean? She couldn't be having those feelings, could she?

She was so wrapped up in her thoughts that when her phone rang ten minutes later, she jumped in her chair and let out a small yelp. She quickly pawed at her phone and answered it.

"Hey, I'm back."

Just hearing Alex's voice sent that little tingle throughout her body again. "Good. So Legs, you're not dripping all over the floor anymore?"

"No, I'm not dripping all over the floor anymore."

Jess laughed. She could hear the eye roll in Alex's voice. "I'm glad to hear that. Now that that's all cleared up, the reason I was calling was to see if you were busy Saturday?"

"Hmmmm…" There was a long pause on the other end. "Saturday, Saturday, let's see…"

Jess was beginning to worry. Maybe she had read the situation wrongly and didn't want to get together, at least not so soon after they had just done so. She was just about to open her mouth when Alex came back on.

"I was just checking my schedule to make sure but as of right now, I don't have anything going on Saturday. What did you have in mind?"

Jess took a deep breath. What did she have to be paranoid about? Alex sounded genuinely excited. "Well…my family heard me talk about you and…not that you have to if you don't want to…but they wanted to invite you, I mean the both of us, to a Saturday barbecue." Talk about the mother of all babbling invitations.

"Oh." The surprise in Alex's voice was more than evident but she quickly continued on. "I'd love to."

"Great." Jess could feel her heart racing as it had when she crossed the finish line during their last 5K. "I'll text you the directions and we can meet there."

"Can't wait."

Hearing those words, Jess wholeheartedly agreed. Saturday seemed like a long way off. "See you then. Good night, Legs."

"Good night, Wheels."

CHAPTER SEVEN

Alex stood on Jess's parents' front porch. Her palm was sweaty as she reached out to knock. This was a big deal. She was meeting *The Family*. Jess wouldn't have wanted to do that if she only saw her as a friend, would she? And as far as that went, how did she feel about the possibility that Jess saw them as becoming more than friends? She had given that a lot of thought over the last couple of days and she kept coming back to the same conclusion. The idea excited her just as Jess excited her in a way that no one had in a long, long time. Just as her knuckles were about to connect with wood, the door whipped open and she was met by Jess's wide smile.

"I see you made it okay, Legs."

"Yep, it wasn't hard at all, Wheels."

"Good, come on in." Jess wheeled back and waved her inside. "Make yourself at home. They're all out on the deck talking and sipping drinks."

Alex stepped through the door and quickly glanced around. The house was set up much like Jess's, with everything arranged

to make it easy for Jess to get around. The level of support that Jess's family showed her was touching. If only her family had shown a fraction of that support.

"Come on, let's head out back. Everyone's dying to meet you."

Why would that be? She felt teary. What had Jess said about her? And what was everyone expecting—Jess's friend or Jess's *girlfriend*? All she could do was smile and hold out her arm. "Lead the way."

Out on the deck, Jess introduced her family. "Alex, this is my mom, Linda Bolderson. Over by the grill is my dad, Pete. This young guy here is my brother-in-law, Tim Poremski." She lowered her voice and leaned closer to Alex. "He's a lawyer but don't hold that against him."

"Always the joker, Jess." Tim rolled his eyes, unperturbed.

Jess continued. "And this is my little sister, Jordan. She's a snot but we still love her."

Jordan stuck out her tongue at Jess, seeming to confirm her sister's assessment.

Finally, Jess turned to Alex with bright smile. "Everyone, this is Alex Hartway."

Jordan sprang from her chair as if launched from a cannon. She ran up and threw her arms around Alex. "Alex. It's so good to have you here."

Alex froze, her entire body stiff, and then she relaxed patting Jordan on the back. Talk about a greeting. She wasn't sure who was more excited for her to be there, Jordan or Jess. "Um… yeah, glad to be here."

Linda called over. "Now Jordan, don't be smothering our guest."

Jordan backed up with a sheepish grin. She looked so much like Jess it was disconcerting. Alex had no doubt that Jess would have been within an inch of Jordan for height. "Sorry Mom. Just welcoming Alex." Jordan bounced back to her chair and flopped down, still beaming.

As nice as it was to see the warm familiar dynamics, Alex felt a pang. It had been nearly fifteen years since she had last

seen her family. Her little brother would be close to Jordan's age, no longer the gangly eleven-year-old she remembered, but a man. And what of her younger sister? Had she grown up to be a vivacious young woman like Jordan? Were either of them married? Then there was her mom and dad. Would she recognize them? They had once been a close family like Jess's, at least she thought they had. Hadn't they loved each other? Hadn't she done everything she could to win her mom and dad's approval—all but one thing?

Looking concerned, Jess peered over at her. "Are you okay?"

Alex swallowed. She hadn't realized that meeting the Boldersons would hit her so hard. It had been years since she had thought about her own family. She forced a smile and nodded. "Yeah, I guess I'm not used to this sort of thing…" Not knowing what else to say, she merely shrugged.

Jess wheeled closer and laid her hand gently on Alex's arm. "It's hard sometimes, isn't it, not having a family?"

Jess had read her mind. As much as she hated them for abandoning her in that anti-gay hellhole laughingly called a treatment center, they were still her family and try as she might to forget, she still missed them. She took a deep breath and covered Jess's hand with hers, giving it a gentle pat. "Yeah, sometimes it is. I try my best not to think about it but then I'll see a family like yours, happy and loving, and I don't know whether I'm jealous, angry, sad or what."

Jess pulled her in close. "Tell you what, whenever you're feeling lonely, you can always borrow my family. They're all clinically insane but they mean well and I'm sure they'll welcome you in with open arms."

All Alex could do was stare down at Jess. She swallowed hard, tears threatening as she stood there. Finally, she leaned in close, her voice low and ragged. "That has to be the nicest offer I've ever had."

* * *

Jess followed her mom into the house to fetch plates and silverware, leaving Alex to chat with Jordan and Tim. Her father stood in front of the grill, carefully tending his speciality—spicy barbecued chicken. Although she was greatly looking forward to her dad's cooking, she was even more excited to see how quickly Alex had fit right in with her family.

Linda grabbed a stack of plates from the cupboard and turned around to place them on Jess's lap. "Your friend certainly seems to be getting along well with Jordan and Tim."

Jess glanced back over her shoulder just in time to catch Alex rolling her head back and laughing. "Yeah, she is. I'm really glad too. I don't think Alex has a lot of close friends."

Linda nodded as she rummaged through the silverware drawer. "She does seem really nice, not at all how Jordan first made her out to be."

Jess laughed, shaking her head. "That was my fault. The first time I met Alex, it didn't go well. She had been having a bad day and I may have been a little overly sensitive—"

"What, you overly sensitive? I can't imagine. That doesn't sound like you at all." With a deeply wry smile, Linda stacked the silverware on the plates in Jess's lap, before patting her on the shoulder.

"Okay, maybe I deserved that." There was no point arguing it—she *was* the hothead of the family. "Anyhow, I had told Jordan about the first time we met and you know Jordan, protective as always. But Alex isn't like that. She's actually really sweet."

"I can see that." Linda turned around and leaned back against the counter. "Not that it's probably any of my business, but what was going on earlier just after you made introductions? Alex seemed upset. Did we do something?"

"No Mom, it was nothing like that." Jess took a deep breath, wondering how much she should share. She wasn't in the habit of keeping things from her family. They had always been fairly open with each other, especially since her accident. As much as she hated to admit it, there were things that she simply didn't have the luxury to keep to herself. One of the biggest annoyances about being in the chair, aside from the most

obvious, were the chronic health issues. Of course she was as health-conscious as she could be, exercising regularly and eating well. But that didn't prevent a whole host of complications due to her paralysis—pressure ulcers from sitting in the chair all day, muscle contracture and atrophy, bone loss and her all-time favorite, urinary tract infections. She could count on one at least every three or four months.

But this was different. Alex had told her about her past in confidence. Still, she didn't want her mom to worry or get the wrong impression. "Alex had a rough time growing up. Her family is very conservative, and they kicked her out when she was eighteen and she came out. Seeing our family reminded her of her family and what she had lost."

Linda winced and covered her mouth with her hand. "That's so sad, Jess. I can't believe any parent would do that to their child."

"There're a lot of crazy people out there fueled by hate and fear." Jess ground her teeth.

"I hope you never felt that way about us."

"No Mom, not even once. You guys were great about everything."

"Thank you." Linda beamed. "But I'll be honest, it wasn't easy at first."

"I don't imagine. It must've been a real shock."

Linda chuckled softly. "Not as much of a shock as you probably thought."

Jess felt her mouth drop open. She had always assumed that no one had suspected. Apparently, she had been wrong…very wrong.

Linda chuckled again. "I know you'd like to think you kept everything hidden but thinking back, it was pretty obvious. You never had any interest in boys, not like Jordan, and even your dear old mom was able to put two and two together with all your Melissa Etheridge and Indigo Girls posters on your wall."

Jess felt as if she had just stepped into the *Twilight Zone* version of her troubled teen years. If only she had known, how different things might've been. "Why didn't you say something?"

Linda shrugged. "We always figured you would tell us if and when you were ready. I didn't want you to feel self-conscious about anything."

"But Mom…" She didn't know what but she felt she had to say something. All these years, she'd been under the impression that her family hadn't had a clue when in fact it had been her that hadn't had a clue. "…I always thought…"

"I won't pretend that we weren't concerned but not because you are gay. We were concerned, as any parent should be, for your safety and well-being. As you said, 'there's a lot of crazy people out there.'"

All Jess could do was stare at her mom in disbelief.

"Plus, there's a lot worse things that could happen to a child than being gay." Linda quickly glanced down at Jess's chair, reached out and gently patted her on the back.

"You're right about that, Mom. There are definitely a lot worse things." Jess could feel her eyes fill with tears. Before her accident, being gay may have been the biggest thing in her life. But afterward, not so much. If only Alex's family could see it from that perspective.

"Just so you know, your friend Alex is always welcome here, no matter what."

Suddenly that lump in her throat seemed much larger. "Thanks…Thanks, Mom. That means a lot…to both of us."

* * *

Alex leaned back in the Adirondack chair, letting the sun beat down on her face. Jess had disappeared in the house to use the bathroom. In the meantime, she was enjoying the beautiful day. If she let herself, she could take a nap. The barbecued chicken was delicious but she had overindulged, leaving her feeling sluggish and sleepy. But what was so wrong with that? It was a lazy Saturday afternoon.

Jordan flopped down in the chair beside her and scooted it closer. "How're you doing?"

How *was* she doing? She hadn't experienced such a convivial family gathering in a very long time, even if she were an adopted member. She did miss it. Finally, she turned to Jordan with a smile. "I'm actually doing great. Thanks for making me feel so at home."

Jordan simply waved her off. "Believe me, it's no biggie." She leaned in even closer, dropping her voice. "I was hoping to talk to you—privately."

Alex perked up, no longer feeling sleepy. What could Jess's little sister want to talk to her privately for? Hopefully, she wasn't like Jess's friend, Terra. She still didn't think she could be in the same room as her without Terra glaring at her and giving off that *die-die-die* vibe. Cautiously, she leaned forward. "Okay…What is it?"

Jordan glanced quickly over her shoulder as if to make sure they weren't going to be overheard. She turned back to Alex. "I just wanted to say that I think you're really good for Jess."

Alex was surprised. She hadn't been expecting that. "Um… thanks." She didn't know what else to say.

"Please, it's us who should thank you. This is the first time since…" Jordan bobbed her head as if searching for words. "… well since I don't know when that I've seen Jess interested in someone. You know, like *really* interested in someone."

She tried to wrap her mind around what Jordan had just said. Jess *interested* in her? She had known that they were getting quite close. And yes, Jess occupied her thoughts almost all the time now. But hearing that information from Jordan made her heart quicken in a way that surprised her. "I'm glad to hear that. I like Jess too."

"I thought so. It was pretty obvious from looking at you." Now Jordan became serious. "But there's something you need to know. Up until now, Jess has avoided any sort of romance or relationship like the plague."

Before she could respond, Jordan continued.

"Ever since her accident, I don't think Jess has felt she could have that." Jordan shook her head. "Don't ask me why. I've told her again and again that she should find someone but she always point-blank refused the possibility."

What Jordan was saying was making a lot of sense to Alex. She had noticed that Jess seemed to be hesitant about the possibility of making a friend. Of course, she hid it behind snarkiness but it was there nonetheless. She had thought that it was due to her initial grossly insensitive comments but maybe there was more to it. "Now that you mention it, I have noticed that a bit but I can understand why. If I were in her place, I'd probably do the same."

Jordan's face lit up, a wide smile slowly lifting the corners of her lips. "That's why I think you're *perfect* for Jess."

Alex could feel her face growing warmer and it had nothing to do with the bright sun beating down. "I...I don't know about that."

"Well, I do. Jess needs someone who is not only understanding but will challenge her like you did at that race. She needs someone who will look at her without being patronizing or treating her as if she's unable to do things."

Alex cringed, their first meeting crystal-clear in her mind. "Jess didn't by chance tell you about the first time we met, did she?"

"Oh, you bet she did." With a laugh, Jordan reached out and clapped Alex on the back. "You should've heard Jess go on. I don't think I've ever heard her cuss a blue streak like that before. We won't even go into what name you were known by for a while."

If her face had been warm before, it was nothing compared to now. Alex wasn't sure if she were more embarrassed or surprised. "I wasn't exactly at my best with that."

"Are you kidding, I think it's great." Jordan again rolled her head back and let out a loud laugh.

"Are you serious?"

"Well, maybe it wasn't great at first but you must admit, you definitely got Jess's attention. And things worked out for the best. So win-win."

"I appreciate what you're saying but..."

"Why am I telling you this? Just so you know the stakes. I think you're good for Jess, you understand what she's been through, and I can tell Jess really likes you. But just be careful."

"Careful? Careful of what?"

"Jess is not as tough as she pretends to be. I don't need to tell you how much an accident like hers can change someone. As much as Jess may seem stubbornly self-assured, I don't think she trusts herself when it comes to romance. Deep down, I think she's worried that somehow she'll never measure up."

"But that's—"

"I know. I feel the same way. But I figured you should know."

Jess came rolling out onto the deck. She looked quickly from Jordan to Alex, her eyebrows rising at the two of them looking guilty. "What's going on? Am I interrupting something?"

Jordan just laughed. "Talk about paranoid—you leave for a few minutes and you think the entire world is conspiring against you."

Jess pursed her lips. "Very funny, ha ha. You know, it's only paranoia if it's not really happening."

Jordan quickly snapped her fingers. "Damn, she's got us. We should have known we couldn't fool her."

If Jess's lips were pursed before, it was nothing compared to the thin white line they had become now. "I swear Jordan...I swear..."

Alex couldn't help but laugh. Although both sisters might look uncannily similar, their personalities couldn't be further apart. Jordan's lackadaisical take-it-as-it-comes outlook on life was in stark contrast to Jess's intensely driven seize-every-moment-for-tomorrow-may-never-come mantra, which probably had a lot to do with her mobility issues. Alex could definitely relate more readily to Jess, not that Jordan wasn't fun to be around. But as Alex watched the two sisters interact, she wondered if she would have shared the same close relationship with her little sister.

Jordan jumped up and scooted her chair to the side. "There, I'll leave the two of you be." With that, she casually sashayed over to Tim and sat on his lap.

Jess wheeled up closer to Alex, still watching Jordan. "I hope Jordan wasn't bugging you too much. You'll have to forgive her. She's never learned the concept of boundaries."

"Don't worry, she was nothing but nice." Alex looked at Jordan who was laughing with her head rolled back and her arms around her husband's neck. She turned to Jess, meeting her eyes. There was strength in those eyes, a fierce determination, a will so strong that Alex felt her breath catch. Jess *exuded* strength. But at what cost? Had it taken losing her legs to bring that out in her? Or had Jess always shown such character? Had losing her own family caused her to push herself the way she did in everything from college to career to even her personal life? Without those life-changing events, would they have turned out differently? And if so, would that have been better? But as she stared deeper into Jess's eyes, beginning to lose herself, what did it matter? Regardless of the past, regardless of the possibilities, they were there together and that was what mattered.

* * *

As the wonderful afternoon wound down, Jess hated to see it end. The highlight had been when her dad had pulled Alex aside to show her the features of his new John Deere lawnmower. To her credit, Alex had been a good sport, listening with interest as her dad pointed out its four-wheel steering. And her mom had treated Alex as if she were a long-lost daughter, constantly offering either more food or refills on her drink. Even Tim had joined in by drumming up a bit of rivalry between Alex's alma mater, Michigan State, and his, University of Michigan. All in all, it had been a great success.

They finally made their goodbyes, everyone seeming reluctant for the afternoon to come to a close. Facing each other beside their cars, Alex shuffled from one foot to the other. "I had a great time. Thanks for inviting me."

Jess looked up into her face. "So did I. Thanks for coming."

The moment drew out. Jess swallowed. She could feel her heartbeat race. Slowly, she licked her lips.

"Do you—" They both spoke at once.

They quickly looked at each other. "You go—" Again, they spoke the exact same words at the exact same time.

They burst out laughing. It had been a long time since Jess had felt that relaxed and free around someone. Even with Terra, God bless her, the best friend she could ever want, she never felt as comfortable around her as she did with Alex. Finally, she wiped away the dampness from the corners of her eyes. "I was just going to ask—"

"Do you want to do something?" Alex jumped right in.

That had been exactly what she was about to ask. "Yeah, do you want to do something? I mean, you don't have to or anything. I was just asking…if you weren't…"

"I'd love to." Alex leaned down and gently laid her hand on Jess's arm. "What do you have in mind?"

Alex's hand against her skin burned like a hot coal from the barbecue. In stark contrast to the warmth of Alex's touch, shivers ran up Jess's arm and throughout her body. She stared up at Alex. Whatever thoughts had been in her head were long gone. All she could do was continue to stare, slowly losing herself in Alex's deep blue eyes while her mouth worked unsuccessfully to form words. Finally, she settled on "Do you want to come back to my place and maybe grab some coffee?" She immediately winced. How lame was that?

Alex cocked her head to the side. "I don't know. It might be a bit late for coffee…"

Jess felt her shoulders drop. Not only had she chosen the worst pickup line in the world, Alex didn't even want coffee.

Seeing Jess's crestfallen look, Alex smiled. "…but I would love to come back to your place. Just no coffee."

Jess suddenly perked up. If she weren't in a wheelchair, she would probably have jumped up and down. Alex was coming back to her place. She didn't have a clue what they would do, but *Alex was coming back to her place*. "Great. I'm sure I can find something besides coffee. I do have wine."

Alex smiled ear to ear. "Wine will do nicely. Should I follow you or…?"

Jess was so shocked that Alex had agreed that at first she couldn't figure out what she was talking about. *Follow her or…?* Then it dawned on her—they had driven separately. What was with her? If her head was any further up in the clouds, she would

need an oxygen mask. "Oh yeah. You should probably follow me, that way you can go straight home from there."

"Sounds like a plan." Alex leaned in. "Just so you know, this isn't a race. I don't think either of us would do too well if it turned into a scene out of *The Fast and the Furious.*"

Jess laughed. "No, probably not. I don't think I can afford to bail us out of jail if we get caught."

"Me either. Plus my car would probably look like me after that 5K by the time we got there."

"You think that's bad? Try street racing with only hand controls."

"Maybe we should just take it easy for once."

"You may be right. So, are you ready, Legs?"

"As I'll ever be, Wheels."

Thirty minutes later, they rolled up in front of Jess's house. Jess opened up her car door and began fishing her chair out from behind her seat. Alex quickly ran up. "Can I help with that?"

Although touched by the gesture, Jess flatly refused the offer. "I'll get it." She hadn't realized how fierce her voice had been until she saw Alex's shocked look. And was there something else there also? Maybe a brief look of hurt? Jess mentally kicked herself. She had fought so long for independence, that it was hard for her to accept any sort of help from anyone. All Alex was doing was trying to be nice. She hadn't deserved her admonition. She turned from her chair half hanging out of her car and looked up at Alex. "I'm sorry, I didn't mean to sound like such a bitch."

"No, I get it. I didn't mean to step on your toes..."Alex blushed. "So to speak of course."

If she hadn't felt like two inches tall before, she certainly did now. Alex was taking the blame. Jess took a deep breath. "You didn't, and I appreciate the offer...I really do. I guess I've been fighting for so long, I don't really know how to let others in." And not just with help, she thought.

Alex kneeled down and took her leather-gloved right hand in hers. "Hey, I'm here no matter what. If I ever overstep my

bounds or do anything to make you uncomfortable, let me know. This is new for both of us."

Jess felt a warmth somewhere deep inside, starting in the pit of her stomach and radiating out. *This is new for both of us.* She liked the sound of that but what exactly was *this* that Alex was referring to—their time together, their friendship, or something more? As if to answer that, Alex quickly leaned in and kissed her gently on the forehead. When Alex pulled back, her eyes glistened in the warm light of the setting sun. Jess stared into those eyes for a moment, a thousand thoughts spinning through her head. Before she could focus on any one of them, she reached out, wrapped her gloved hand around the back of Alex's neck and pulled her in. This time their lips met, tentatively at first, then with increasing passion, increasing hunger.

Jess lost all track of time. Had it been a minute…an hour… more? She didn't know. What's more, she didn't care. It could have been a day for all she knew and it wouldn't have mattered a bit. How long had it been since she had felt like this? Actually, the night before her accident. She hadn't realized how much she had missed, how much she had forced herself to forget. It wasn't until a car horn broke the moment that she finally looked up. Her face turned fifty shades of red as her neighbor, Mrs. O'Connor, drove by. Of any neighbor, it had to be the nosy one. She met Alex's eyes, her face red too—or was it the light from the sunset? They both fell into wild laughter.

"Wow, where did that come from?"

Alex shrugged. "I don't know but I think I liked it."

"Yeah, me too." Jess took both of Alex's hands in hers and gave them a firm squeeze. "What do you say we go inside before we scandalize the neighborhood even more."

Alex quickly glanced over her shoulder, a panicked looked suddenly on her face. "This isn't going to cause you any trouble, is it?"

Jess didn't need to be a psychic to read Alex's thoughts. She was thinking about her family and how they had abandoned her. She gave her hands another firm squeeze. "Don't worry about it. No one in this neighborhood cares about that." She laughed.

"Not that Mrs. O'Connor won't gossip. She'll gossip no matter what but not because of that. She's not nasty, just a busybody with nothing better to do. No one pays her any mind."

"You sure? I don't want to cause you any trouble."

Jess hooked a thumb over her shoulder to the rainbow flag flying from her porch. "Besides, if they couldn't figure it out by the flag by now…"

The tension drained from Alex as she relaxed. "Good."

"All the same, what do you say we head on in? Once inside, Jess waved her arms wide. "Make yourself at home. *Mí Casa Su Casa* and all that."

"Thanks." Alex walked over to the living room couch and sat down.

Jess wheeled up in front of her. "Can I get you anything to drink? I know I offered wine but I also have water, orange juice, tea, beer."

At the mention of beer, Alex raised her eyebrows. "Beer, huh?"

"You bet! I have Murphy's and Murphy's."

Alex chuckled, a soft rolling sound coming from her lips. "In that case, I'll go with Murphy's."

"Murphy's it is. Be right back." Jess zipped into the kitchen and grabbed two English pub glasses, dropped them into her lap, and then grabbed two cans of Murphy's from the fridge. As almost an afterthought, she snatched the bag of chips from the counter. It may not have been the healthiest snack, but how often did she have company?

She quickly wheeled back into the living room where she handed Alex her beer and a glass. She tossed the bag of chips onto the couch and set her empty glass and can of beer on the end table before sliding herself from her chair to the couch. Although she had done it thousands of times before, it was still a precarious maneuver. There was always the possibility of spilling herself onto the floor instead. "What do you say we pick out a movie or something on cable?"

Alex smiled, foam mustache clinging to her top lip. "Sounds good to me."

Jess grabbed the remote—BBC America lit up the screen. They both turned to each other and at the same time cried out, "*Dr. Who!*"

"I had no idea you were a *Dr. Who* fan," said Alex excitedly.

"Are you kidding? My other chair is a TARDIS."

Alex stared at her as the words sank in. She rolled her head back and let out a loud, snorting laugh. "Oh my God, I can't believe you said that. That's hilarious!"

"You like, huh?" Jess had a smile so wide that her cheeks were smarting. She had never found anyone before that thought her *Dr. Who* joke was that funny. Not even her co-workers at the bookstore and they were the biggest bunch of geeks and nerds she had ever met.

Alex fixed her eyes on her, her head slightly lowered. "I do."

From Alex's look, Jess wasn't sure that she was talking about her joke—at least not entirely. There was a whole lot more there. Before she could lose her nerve, she quickly scooted across the couch and wrapped her arm around Alex's shoulders, gently pulling her close until their foreheads touched. Her voice was low, not much more than a whisper. "I like it also."

She leaned in, her breath growing more ragged with every second. This was it, no turning back now. But was she ready? Was anyone ever fully ready? Ten years—it had been too long. And what did it matter? At that moment, all she could think about was the steamy heat coming from Alex's breath, the quiver of her body as it pressed up against hers, the roaring of her heart. Millimeter by millimeter they moved closer. Her entire body—at least what she could feel—tingled as if electricity was dancing over the surface of her skin. For the first time since her accident, she felt fully alive, complete. At last, at long last, their lips met and she was whole.

What started as slow and sensual quickly turned passionate, hot, frantic. Jess gasped breath after rapid breath between frenzied kisses. It had been so long since she had allowed herself to let go. She still wasn't sure it was a good idea but whatever warning her brain was whispering, it was drowned out by a deeper, lower, louder voice. She wouldn't have been able to

stop even if she wanted to. And that was what surprised her the most—she didn't want to stop, not now, not ever.

She slowly ran her gloved hands over Alex's body, starting at her shoulders and working down her arms, over her sides, and up again. When she reached Alex's neck, she cupped her hand behind Alex's head, her fingers twisting in Alex's hair, and pulled her in tight, forcing their lips together even more. Alex let out a long, low moan that she swallowed. Jess felt her heart thunder. Forget about races, this was all the exercise she would ever need.

The thought struck her funny but a laugh froze in her throat as she felt Alex's fingers dip under the hem of her shirt and work up her bare skin. Jess gasped and Alex immediately pulled back, breaking their kiss.

"Oh God, Jess, I'm sorry. I don't know what I was thinking. I didn't mean…"

At the panicked look on Alex's face, Jess quickly silenced her with a thumb stroking the edge of Alex's mouth. "Shhh. Alex, trust me, it's okay. You haven't done anything wrong. I was just a little surprised, that's all. It's been a long, long time since someone's touched me like that. I guess it caught me off guard."

Alex relaxed. "Still, I should have talked to you first."

Jess laughed. "And ruin the spontaneity. Alex, really, it's fine." She quickly hooked her fingers under the hem of her shirt, pulled it over her head and tossed it on the couch behind her. Just as quickly, she removed her black lace bra.

This time, Alex gasped. "Jess, are you sure?" She stared at Jess's bare skin, her small breasts high on her muscular chest.

"Legs, if I weren't, I wouldn't be sitting beside you topless."

With a smile, Alex slowly nodded. "You make a good point, Wheels."

"You'd better believe it. Now I believe fair's fair." She fixed Alex's shirt with her eyes and jerked her head up quickly twice. Fair definitely was fair.

Without removing her eyes from Jess, Alex reached down and slowly lifted her shirt. Jess bit her lip as more and more skin was exposed. Alex was taking her time, teasing, but if she didn't hurry, Jess might just have to help out and if that were the case,

she couldn't guarantee what condition Alex's shirt would be in when she was done.

Finally, *finally*, Alex lifted her shirt over her breasts, pulling it along with her sports bra the rest of the way in a quick, fluid motion. Jess again gasped. She stared at Alex's breasts as they jiggled slightly with her movement, rising and falling with each breath Alex took. She hadn't realized how beautiful Alex was. Of course, she had caught glances and imagined what Alex might look like, but none of that compared to the beauty before her.

In contrast with her own dark nipples, Alex's were pale pink, puckered and erect. Her skin was light and creamy with a cute triangle of freckles between and over the inner swell of her breasts breaking up the otherwise flawless skin. She licked her lips. Those freckles beckoned. Jess slowly removed the black glove from her left hand, working the leather over her knuckles and sliding her fingers free. With her left hand naked, she stripped the glove from the right—slowly, slowly, like a sensual hand striptease. She tossed the gloves over her shoulder and leaned forward, first cupping Alex's left breast and then her right in her bare hands.

Alex arched her back, caressing Jess's naked flesh at the same time. Slowly, Jess worked her hands over Alex's chest, lifting her breasts and pushing them together before letting them gently fall and starting all over again. She massaged them in circles— once, twice, three times—never once taking her eyes from Alex's peaked nipples.

Alex swirled her thumb over Jess's nipple, sending a shudder through Jess's body. Jess bit her lip. She was light-headed. This was what she had been missing, all these years. She lowered her lips to Alex's right nipple and drew it in over her teeth, giving it a playful nip. Alex quickly sucked in a breath through her closed teeth. Jess closed her eyes. It had been far, *far* too many years.

CHAPTER EIGHT

Alex couldn't believe how easily they had segued from friends to something more—something much more. It had already been over two weeks since their first kiss. And what a kiss! She smiled at the thought. It wasn't just the kiss either. They had stayed up all night, talking, laughing, watching *Dr. Who* and kissing some more. A lot more. It was all she could do to tear herself away from Jess the next day but she had to work that night.

And although their intimacy hadn't progressed beyond breast play, she didn't mind. If that was all they were able to do, all that Jess felt comfortable with, she didn't care. When she looked at Jess, when she was *with* Jess, she didn't see any limitations. She certainly didn't *feel* any limitations. She would take Jess for whatever she could give.

Even as she bounced around the ER, she couldn't shake the feeling of walking on air. And it hadn't gone unnoticed either. She hadn't been on the floor twenty minutes before Maria flagged her down.

"Someone's certainly in a good mood tonight." Maria eyed her up and down, a devilish grin lighting up her face.

"What's not to be in a good mood about? It's a beautiful day." She had aimed for indifference, failing miserably.

Maria pursed her lips. "Nice try, Doc, but you'll have to get up a lot earlier in the morning to fool this old bird. Now out with it. Did someone get lucky this weekend?"

Alex felt her face immediately blush bright red. Only Maria could get away with such a question. That was why she loved her so much—there was no pretense with Maria. "I'm not one to kiss and tell but I did have a very nice weekend."

"Uh-huh" Maria gave a curt nod as if she had known all along. "This wouldn't be that young woman you ran that race with a couple of weeks back, would it?"

"Actually, it would."

"I'd ask you how things are going but the look on your face says it all. She must be special."

"She is." Alex wouldn't've thought it possible, but Maria had actually made her color even more. So much keeping it hidden.

Besides Maria, she had been complimented over the last two weeks by the rest of the staff and even several of her patients. It was hard to believe that had made such a difference but Jess had certainly brought out the best in her.

When not at the hospital, she spent the evenings at Jess's. Weather permitting, they would stroll up and down the White Pine Trail. On the odd night when the weather chased them indoors, they curled up on the couch and passed the time together watching sci-fi on TV. Other than the night when they had first kissed though, she hadn't spent the night again. She wasn't really sure why either. Jess had seemed nervous about the prospect of a sleepover, even if that didn't particularly mean sleeping together. And to be fair, she was more than a little nervous herself.

She would've liked to invite Jess over to her house but that would prove nearly impossible. She never realized how many steps she had until she looked at it through Jess's eyes. Fifteen steps leading up to the front door, and three steps up from

her sunken living room. And that didn't include the stairway upstairs or the five steps down to the rear deck. It had been a selling point—get some exercise by walking around the house, a workout for her glutes without even trying. But now, it was a ton of inconvenient obstacles that prevented her from sharing her home life with Jess.

If things continued to go as well as they had been—she crossed her fingers—then sometime in the near future she was going to have to make some hard decisions concerning her housing. But what would Jess think about that? That was a big step, a *very* big step. She certainly didn't want to overwhelm her and scare her away.

But there would be time for that. All she was concerned about tonight was getting to Jess's as soon as possible. For the third time in as many minutes, she glanced down at her speedometer and had to ease off the gas. Five miles an hour over, even ten wasn't a big deal. Twenty over—the last thing she needed was a speeding ticket.

Finally, in what seemed like hours but in reality had only been about twenty-five minutes, she pulled up in front of Jess's house. She grabbed the bag of groceries and quickly ran up the path. She hit the porch as the front door opened, Jess was waiting there with a wide smile. She bent down and kissed Jess, quickly at first then lingering longer and longer.

Jess broke the kiss first, still smiling ear to ear. "Why don't you come on in before we scandalize the entire neighborhood." She let out a soft laugh then grabbed the groceries from Alex's hands.

"I can get that."

"Don't be silly, Legs. You've been on your feet all day." Jess dropped the bag onto her lap.

"Oh har har, very funny, Wheels. And I don't suppose your hands have had a break all day either." They could happily joke back and forth. She had come to think of Jess's chair as simply an aspect of her.

"My hands are tougher than your feet."

Of that, she had no doubt. Jess's hands were hands-down—no pun intended—tougher than her feet any day.

Jess wheeled toward her kitchen. "I hope you're hungry."

"Starving."

"Good, because I'm going to make the best stir-fry you've ever had."

In anticipation, Alex's stomach gave an almighty growl.

After dinner, they retired to Jess's back deck, NPR playing in the background, the shadows growing longer. As quickly as the daylight was fading, crickets and frogs began their twilight serenade. Alex turned to Jess, a soft smile on her lips. She reached out and took her gloved hand in hers, giving it a gentle, reassuring squeeze. "I could do this forever."

"Me too, but…" Jess let out a long, drawn-out sigh.

"But…?" She leaned in closer, not taking her eyes off Jess.

Jess stared down into her lap. She swallowed once and then again with difficulty. Finally, she cleared her throat but still her voice was ragged. "I love what we have—what seems to be growing between us. I never thought I could feel this way about someone, not after…well, you know…now. But here we are. Half the time, I feel like I'm living in some dream and any moment, I'll wake up. The rest of the time, I feel that if it *is* a dream then it's one where I never want to wake up. I'm sorry, I'm probably not making any sense."

Alex reached over and gently caressed Jess's cheek. The smooth, soft feel of Jess's skin against her hand sent a tremor up her arm and through the rest of her body. Her voice was not much more than a whisper. "Actually, it makes perfect sense. That's how I feel too."

Jess looked up, meeting Alex's gaze. A small, tentative smile touched her lips. "I haven't felt this happy in a long, long time. I just want you to know that." Whatever smile had been there quickly faded. "But…"

"But? But what?" Alex bit her bottom lip as she waited. Jess was obviously struggling with something. Hopefully, she hadn't done something to upset her. That was her greatest fear—that

somehow through her ignorance, she would do something that would hurt Jess. "Did I do something wrong?"

Jess's eyes grew as wide as miniatures of the full moon gleaming overhead. Her mouth opened in shock. "No Alex. Oh God, no. I don't want you to think that. You haven't done anything wrong."

Alex was confused. What could Jess possibly be agonizing about? She spun around so she could face Jess directly, taking both her hands in hers and scooting in close. "Hon, whatever it is just talk to me and we can work it out."

Jess took a deep breath, searching for her words. Finally, when she looked up, her misty eyes were sparkling in the moonlight. "I swore I would never get involved with someone, and then you came along." She tilted her head with a wry smile, however there was nothing bitter in her expression. "In the past few weeks, you've become a huge part of my life. And that scares me more than a little."

"But why would that scare you?" Overhead, clouds scuttled across the sky. Alex watched as the shadows played across Jess's face, a panoply of emotions.

Jess sucked in another deep breath. She peered into Alex's eyes, almost pleading. A cloud shifted, bathing her face in bright moonlight. A line sparkled on each cheek where two fat tears slowly crawled their way down her smooth skin. Alex reached up and gently brushed them away, cradling Jess's chin in her hands. She pulled Jess in, her head resting on her shoulder, her fingers brushing through her short dark hair. "Shhh…shhh… it'll be all right. It'll be all right."

Alex wasn't sure how long they stayed like that—five minutes, ten, twenty? All she wanted was to hold Jess and somehow show her that what she said was true. *It'll be all right.* If only she could be sure. At the moment, she didn't even know what was wrong. How could she be sure that everything would be all right? Somehow, she just knew.

Finally, Jess pulled back. Her cheeks shimmered in the soft moonlight. "Alex, you're so sweet. You really deserve someone who can be a complete woman for you."

Now it dawned on her. Now she knew. This was about Jess being in a wheelchair. But how could Jess feel that way? She thought they had gone beyond that. Had she done something, anything, to make her think that? She opened her mouth but no words came out.

Jess smiled sadly, the look in her eyes heart-wrenching. "I can never be that for you. I know I should have said this earlier. I never should have—"

"I want you."

Jess froze, her mouth hanging open. She looked as if she had been slapped. Several moments ticked by before she blinked. "But—"

"I want you." Alex said it again, this time with a firm nod.

Jess blinked. "Oh Alex, how can you say that? Can't you see—?"

Alex again cut her off. "Of course I can *see*. I *see* a beautiful young woman who has set my heart on fire. I *see* someone with a determination so fierce that all I can do is simply stare in astonishment. I *see* someone who brings out the best in me. I *see* someone I can picture spending the rest of my life with, getting to know her more and more each day."

Jess began to cry again softly, large silent tears running down her cheeks. "Of course you say that now but what happens later on? I can never be a whole woman for you. I can never be with you in the way another woman can. You're forgetting that I can't feel my legs, that I can't feel anything from my hips down."

Alex reached out, her hands pressed firmly to Jess's damp cheeks. She stared directly into Jess's deep dark eyes. "Hon, I don't care about that. I want to be with you in any way I can. So there might be some aspects of intimacy that are not available to us. Who cares? As long as I'm with *you*"—she gave Jess a gentle shake—"you hear me, as long as I'm with you, that's all that matters. Besides, there's a lot more to intimacy than what's below someone's waist."

Jess threw herself forward and wrapped her arms tightly around Alex. She pulled her face in close and pressed her lips to Alex's ear. "You had better mean that, Legs."

Alex pulled back enough to again stare directly into Jess's eyes. "Always, Wheels. Always."

Jess took Alex by the hand and led her into the house to the couch. As Alex sat, Jess slipped from her chair, pulling herself up beside Alex. With a smile, Jess quickly peeled off her shirt while Alex followed suit. Alex pulled Jess to her, their lips meeting. Only a few minutes passed before they both pulled back, gasping.

"That never gets old." Jess's chest heaved.

"It certainly doesn't. I could do that forever with you." Alex fought for breath.

"Me too, Legs. Me too." Biting her bottom lip, Jess slowly removed her gloves. Alex swallowed, watching Jess. No matter how many times she had seen Jess remove her gloves, it was still the hottest thing she had ever seen, even more so than seeing Jess topless, as strange as that sounded. This was the one part of herself that Jess never showed anyone but her.

Jess lightly tossed the gloves on the end table and brought her hand to Alex, cradling her face with Alex's cheek resting in her palm. Alex closed her eyes. The sensation sent shivers throughout her body. She could feel her arousal building more and more every second. Warm, then hot, then burning. Jess slowly traced her soft palm over Alex's skin, the feeling so different from the leather touch that Alex had grown accustomed to. It was all she could do not to grab Jess's hand and plunge it where it was needed the most but she let Jess take her time.

As Jess worked her hands ever lower, passing over her shoulder and to her chest, Alex leaned in, pressing her lips to Jess's. She took Jess's left breast into her hand, rubbing, massaging, caressing. She broke their kiss to mouth Jess's right nipple, freshly hard and erect. The salty sweetness of Jess's skin made her stomach stir. Or maybe it was Jess's hand as she rubbed her lower abs, the muscles jumping with every soft touch.

When Jess reached the top edge of her jeans, Alex felt Jess's fingers pause between the fabric and her skin. Jess slowly tickled her fingertips along that edge, sending shivers through Alex's body and raising goose bumps on her overly sensitive skin. Every nerve was firing all at once. Jess's fingers tentatively

slipped between the fabric and Alex's skin. Alex gasped as her stomach contracted. Her abs were so tight she felt as if she had done a hundred crunches. But just as she thought her eyes were about to roll back in her head, Jess pulled her hand back. A soft whimper escaped Alex's throat as she opened her eyes.

"Are you okay?"

"Yeah. Couldn't be better." Jess smiled shyly. "Only one thing…"

Alex sat up straight. "What? Did I do something wrong? Do you want to stop?"

"No silly. I just need some help with your pants." Jess chuckled, a light musical sound.

"Oh…*Oh*…" Alex felt her face grow warmer. A flush creeped across her skin and she swallowed again. Without taking her eyes from Jess, she unbuttoned her jeans and lifted her butt, slowly working her jeans over her hips, exposing the light blond triangle of fine hair. Once the jeans were free, Alex slid them down her legs until the pant legs bunched at her ankles. In her haste, she somehow twisted her jeans until they locked her legs together in denim ankle cuffs. The more she struggled, the tighter they got. "Shit!"

Jess snorted. "Here, let me help you." She quickly unknotted Alex's jeans and slid them off the rest of the way. Jess leaned back, her hand resting just above Alex's mound. Slowly, she tickled her fingers along the edge of Alex's pubic hair.

Alex sucked in a quick breath and squirmed at the sensation. She could feel every individual hair as Jess's fingers passed, each one sending a jolt through her overstimulated body. The scent of arousal filled the room and Alex felt her wetness grow. She couldn't remember being that wet in a long, long time, if ever. What would Jess think?

Jess moved her fingers lower and Alex let out a deep, guttural moan. Her back arched as Jess's fingertips parted her swollen, throbbing lips.

"Oh my God, Legs, you're so wet."

"Uh-huh." That was all she could manage.

"Mmmmm. I like." Jess gradually picked up speed as she stroked Alex's moist center. She circled her fingertip over Alex's pulsing clitoris and then slipped her fingers inside—deeper, deeper, faster, faster.

Alex clenched her teeth, her back arched. Her breath came in gasps. Her stomach clenched, again and again. How much more could she take?

Jess leaned in, her hot breath against Alex's ear. "Do you want to come for me, Legs?"

"Uh...huh..." Alex groaned out the words, her face contorted.

Jess pressed harder, deeper. "Come for me then, Legs. Come for me."

Hearing those words pushed Alex over the edge. She let out a loud, long, primal moan as wave after wave of pleasure wracked her body. She twisted her fingers into the couch. Tears trickled down her cheeks. She wasn't one to cry during sex. But this was different. This was Jess. This was special in a way that she had never experienced before.

Jess wiped away a tear with her thumb, concern in her eyes. "I didn't mean to make you cry. Are you okay?"

Alex gave her a reassuring smile. "More than okay. I'm perfect."

Jess relaxed. "I know."

Alex reached for Jess, pulling her closer. "Now, it's your turn." She dropped her fingers to the button on Jess's jeans.

Jess gently pushed Alex's hand away, a sad smile on her lips. "That's okay, Legs. I appreciate it but there's really no point when I can't feel anything down there."

Alex felt her heart drop. "Are you sure? I want to return the pleasure."

Jess sighed softly. "Just being here with me, Legs, is all the pleasure I need."

* * *

Long after the sun had set, they continued to sit on the deck talking and reminiscing until the mosquitoes, some the size of small birds, finally chased them inside. Jess grabbed cold drinks from the fridge, while Alex poured salsa in a bowl and opened a fresh bag of Tostitos. They retreated to the living room where Jess turned on the radio. Garrison Keillor's deep, rich voice filled the room. Jess set the cans of soda on the end table and slid herself from her chair to the couch.

"You need any help there?"

"Nope, I got it." Jess made a conscious effort not respond with a biting retort. She smiled to herself. Old habits die hard. She could see now that Alex asked simply because she cared—no other motivation, no other agenda, no other reason. With that thought, she gave Alex a warm, wide smile. "Thanks though."

"Anytime." Alex flashed a bright smile back at her.

Now settled, Jess handed Alex a can of Diet Coke and cracked open the other, taking a long, refreshing drink. They spent the next minutes in companionable silence.

"This is nice."

She reached over and squeezed Alex's hand. "Yes, it is."

Alex scooted closer, laying her hand over the soft leather covering Jess's hand, the one still gripping hers. Very slowly, she lightly brushed her palm up Jess's forearm, back and forth, back and forth. Jess swallowed, her mouth suddenly dry. Her heart pounded in her ears. Her stomach rolled.

As much as she would've liked to have blamed it on the junk food, that simply wasn't the case. And why try to blame it on anything? Shouldn't she enjoy it? Like any other woman? Again, those old habits die hard. She might not be like any other woman but why should that matter? Had she just been telling herself for so long that it *did* matter, that it *did* make a difference, that she couldn't be with someone, that even when the possibility was sitting right beside her, she still found it difficult to accept. She swallowed again.

Alex continued to run her hand back and forth over her arm, tickling her flesh with her fingertips. Jess's skin erupted in goose pimples and a shudder ran through her body. Her head

was light and her body had a heavy, almost drowsy feeling as if she were sinking into the couch.

They drew even closer. Jess looked up, peering deep into Alex's dark blue eyes. She'd never seen eyes so blue, almost a midnight blue. But there was more. Those pools of blue darkness caught the light and sparkled with each slight movement Alex made, with each breath. The deeper Jess looked, the more she felt as if at any moment she could fall into that inky blue abyss. There was only one way to describe it—breathtaking.

Before she knew what was happening, she was in Alex's arms. Their lips met, gently at first and then with increasing urgency. When Alex's lips parted, she took complete advantage, thrusting her tongue inside. Her mouth was no longer dry. She fought for breath but no matter how hard she tried, she couldn't seem to get enough air. Just when she pulled up for a breath, Alex swapped places, thrusting her tongue into her mouth. Back and forth, back and forth, they traded places, each time faster and faster, more forceful, more urgent.

Finally when they pulled apart, Jess sat gasping, her heart racing as if she had just crossed the finish line of a marathon with the best time in her life. She didn't just feel as if she were sinking into the couch anymore, she felt as if she had been poured onto it. Her lips were swollen and tender. Her face felt like an oven. Alex looked disheveled, her hair mussed and a deep flush across her cheeks and down her neck. But it was Alex's eyes, those deep blue infinite pools, that surprised her the most. Jess had never seen such desire in someone's eyes before, especially not toward her. Her heart raced once again.

Concern replaced desire as Alex leaned in. "Are you all right?" Her voice low, soft.

How could she answer that question? *Are you all right?* She wasn't sure. This could be enough, the intimacy they shared, couldn't it? Even with her limitations, she could be a whole woman for Alex, right? Or could she? *Are you all right?* Such an innocuous question. If she wasn't all right, she didn't know if she ever would be. "I…I think so." Her voice cracked on the last word.

Alex quickly stood. "Maybe I should…" She hooked a thumb over her shoulder toward the front door.

Oh great, thought Jess, now Alex has the wrong idea. Jess was at a loss for words. Finally, as Alex took a step backward, she croaked out a single word. "Stay."

Alex shook her head. "I think I should probably be—"

"Alex, please stay." Her voice was soft, pleading. Before Alex could protest again, she took a deep breath, words coming out in a jumble. "Look Alex, I never thought I would say this but please don't go. I want you to stay with me tonight—no expectations, no conditions, no assumptions—just stay."

Alex took a tentative step forward. "Are you sure?"

Jess reached out and took Alex's hands in hers, pulling her in. "Legs, I have never been more sure of anything in my life."

* * *

Alex woke the next morning with Jess in her arms. Sunlight streamed in through the windows, bathing them in a gentle warmth like a wool blanket on a cold winter's day. The soft *coo* of a mourning dove echoed somewhere outside. Alex couldn't ever remember waking up to such a beautiful morning. If not for the rise and fall of Jess's chest against hers, she might have thought it was all a dream. But it wasn't—it had really happened. They hadn't made it any farther than the couch last night. Her back certainly wasn't happy about that. Regardless she couldn't imagine a better evening.

As she lay there, she slowly stroked her hand up and down Jess's leg. It was several minutes before it dawned on her like a slap against the face—Jess couldn't feel that. How easy it was to forget. It wasn't easy for Jess to forget. Every moment, everything she did was a constant reminder. The more she thought about that, the sadder she felt. As much as she may feel sorry for Jess at times, she couldn't share that with her. Jess wanted no sympathy.

Last night had been such a surprise. She had not expected Jess to make that move. Although she still had a lot of questions,

the one thing she was sure of was that no matter what may come, she wanted Jess to be a part of it. What would their relationship be like? What did the future hold for them? She didn't know. All she did know was last night had been an important step in the right direction.

Jess shifted her weight and Alex glanced down at her. Even asleep, Jess had a wide smile on her lips. So beautiful. She reached out and lightly stroked Jess's short brunette bangs. Jess's eyes fluttered and she looked up into Alex's face, her deep brown eyes sparkling in the early morning light and her smile growing wider.

"Good morning, sunshine."

Jess stifled a yawn with the back of her hand. "Good...good morning." She yawned again.

"I didn't mean to wake you." Alex continued to stroke her hair with her thumb.

"No...no that's all right." Jess laughed as she tried her best to fight yet another yawn. "I'm usually a morning person. I don't know why I'm so tired."

"I could think of a reason or two." Alex lifted an eyebrow.

Jess chuckled softly. "I bet. What a night."

"Yes, what a night. No regrets?"

Jess stretched, a grimace on her face. "Only one—I'm too old to sleep on the couch anymore. Whose idea was this anyway?"

"I do believe it was yours."

"Oh, in that case, it was a brilliant idea even if I am stiff as a board."

Alex laughed. "I hear you there. I feel like I've been hit by a truck." The words were barely out of her mouth when she gasped. "Oh my God, Jess. I'm so sorry. I didn't mean to say that." How could she have been so careless?

"Legs..." Jess reached up and pressed her fingers to Alex's lips. "It's okay. I'm not offended."

"I don't know what I was thinking. It just came out."

"Relax. Trust me, it's really no big deal. As one who can personally attest, getting hit by a truck sucks so if you feel that

bad, maybe we should get up." Jess cupped her hand to Alex's cheek and gave her a reassuring smile.

Alex exhaled. She hadn't realized she had been holding her breath. What a stupid thing to say. She might as well have said that after sleeping on the couch, she would need a wheelchair. She more and more saw Jess as a beautiful, strong, energetically alive young woman. Most times, she didn't even notice that Jess was in a wheelchair. She simply saw Jess as Jess, someone for whom she was falling hard and fast. With that thought, she covered Jess's hand against her cheek with her own and returned her smile. "I could actually stay here like this all day with you in my arms."

"Ah Legs, you sure know what to say to a girl." For a moment Jess's eyes turned misty but then she smiled wider. "Tell you what—why don't we get up and I'll fix you my famous world-class breakfast."

"Now you're talking. Pancakes, sausage, bacon—bring it on, I'm starving."

Jess laughed when she saw Alex about to spring up. "Perhaps I have overhyped my breakfast abilities. All I have to offer is scrambled eggs and orange juice. I hope that will be okay."

Looking her deep in the eyes, Alex slowly nodded. "As long as I'm having it with you, it is sure to be perfect."

* * *

Jess rolled into work a little past eleven, two hours past her normal starting time. Since her schedule was pretty flexible, it wasn't a big deal. She would have much rather spent the day with Alex but she had a print run that simply could not wait.

But maybe it was for the best. It would give her a chance to clear her head so she could reflect. She was still coming to terms with its enormity. She had shared a night with someone. *She had made love to someone.* But as amazing as it had been, she couldn't shake the feeling that she had let Alex down. She couldn't be everything for her. Alex couldn't reciprocate. She would always have limitations and that wasn't fair to Alex, wasn't fair to anyone.

She had barely wheeled up to the Espresso when Terra came trotting across the floor. "Jess, there you are. I was beginning to wonder if you were even going to show up today. Are you all right?"

Are you all right? There was that question again, the same question Alex had asked. How on earth could she answer? She and Alex had had sex. It had been amazing. But there was a limitation, no way around it. Finally, she managed a feeble, "oh yeah."

Terra leaned in, obviously concerned. "Are you sure you're okay, Jess? You don't seem yourself. What's going on?"

Great, now she had Terra worried. She was going to have to come clean. "It's nothing, really. I'm just trying to make sense of some things. Alex spent the night with me."

"*What?* You've got to be *kidding* me. What were you thinking?" Terra's voice carried throughout the store, causing a couple of older women in the puzzle section to look up in alarm.

Not exactly the response she needed. As if she didn't have enough on her mind without Terra having a hissy fit. "Whoa, calm down, Terra. What's the big deal?"

"What's the big deal? *What's* the big *deal?* I'll tell you what's the big deal. That Alex is trying…trying to…she's trying to take advantage of you." Terra could barely get her words out, her face turning blotchy purple.

It was no secret that Terra wasn't a fan of Alex. And Jess could understand—Alex had made a rotten first impression. But she had explained that to Terra. She had seemed okay with it. So where was all this coming from? And furthermore, who was Terra to be telling her who she could and could not spend the night with? "Terra, what are you talking about?"

"I'll tell you what I'm talking about. Alex, the good doctor." Terra's words dripped with contempt. "I knew there was something about her I didn't like. What kind of sick—"

"Now hang on right—"

"—sorry piece of—"

"—Hey! That's enough. Terra, I love you but that's uncalled for." Jess bristled. Or what her grandma used to say—she had her Irish up. She might not have the fair skin and red hair but

there were times when she could get her Irish up and this was certainly one of them. Terra was only being protective, for which she was grateful, but she was out of line—*way* out of line. "Alex has been nothing if not sweet to me. And for your information—it was *my* idea for her to stay. I'm happy, happier than I've been in I don't know when. So if you care about me at all, instead of bashing Alex all the time, you could try to be happy for me…for us. If not, then…" She wasn't sure how to finish that but she wasn't going to let anyone rip on Alex.

Terra stared dumbfounded, as if Jess had smacked her. She had never spoken to Terra like that. Terra opened her mouth, gasping. Finally, she took a deep breath. "I'm…I'm sorry, Jess. I didn't mean to…" She slowly lowered her head.

Jess massaged her forehead. She had a blistering headache. "I'm sorry too. I shouldn't have jumped down your throat like that. I know you're only thinking about my wellbeing but seriously, I'm fine…more than fine…and Alex has a lot to do with that. Can't you forgive and forget—I have."

Terra slowly looked up. "I can try but I can't promise anything."

That was better than nothing—baby steps. She had never met someone who could hold a grudge like Terra. "Okay, I'll take that."

When Terra slumped off to the information desk, Jess turned back to her machine. She had a ton of work to do but her heart wasn't in it. She quickly pulled out the schedule and scanned through the job list. Only one small printing had to be done. She could get through that in an hour or two easily.

Finally, as predicted time-wise, she finished up and shut down the book machine. Without saying goodbye to anyone, she punched out and wheeled herself out the back door. She felt a sense of loss. Infinity Books had always been a safe house, an emotional oasis away from the real world. Terra certainly hadn't meant to damage that and she'd be distraught to know that she had caused just that. Thankfully, one thing her life had taught her, tomorrow would be better. And if not…well she could deal with that also.

CHAPTER NINE

"Where have you been hiding yourself, Alex?" Jamie walked out with a bottle of wine and three glasses. "You haven't been avoiding us, have you?"

"Yeah, we haven't seen you forever." Sue chimed in.

"Huh, has it been that long?" Trying her best at innocence, Alex hid a moony smile behind her hand. She had been expecting some good-natured ribbing from her best friends, neglected since she had been spending so much time with Jess. Not that they would care, given the reason.

"As a matter of fact it has." Jamie handed her a glass and poured a wonderful Tabor Hill gewürztraminer. "Does this mean that things are going well with a certain young woman?"

Alex could feel her cheeks beginning to burn. Things were most definitely going well with a certain young woman, more so than she could have ever dreamed. Jess had become a huge part of her life and unless she was mistaken, Jess felt the same way.

Sue waved her hand in front of Alex's face. "Earth to Alex, come in Alex."

Alex blinked. Her cheeks were on fire. She didn't think she could feel more heat if she shoved her head in an oven. At the look on both Jamie and Sue's face, a combination of concern and amusement, she hooted in amusement. "Sorry about that. I must have been daydreaming."

Jamie raised her eyebrows, taking a close look at Alex. "Hmmm, I guess. Must have been some daydream. You look like the cat that ate the canary."

Jamie still looked at her with deep concern. "All joking aside, are you sure you're okay, Alex?"

Alex waved her off. "Yes, I'm okay, better than okay."

They sat around the large patio table that took center stage on Jamie and Sue's back deck. Alex set her wineglass down in front of her. Jamie leaned in with her elbows on the table, a sharp, piercing glint in her eye. "Alex, seriously, what's going on with Jess. I'd have to guess things are going very well."

Alex slowly nodded her head. That was about all she could manage. As much as she wanted to spill everything to Jamie and Sue, she couldn't seem to find the words. Finally, she looked up, a sheepish grin on her lips. "Yes, thing are going great with Jess. We've been hanging out almost every night, that is the nights I'm not working. She really is amazing. I never thought I would meet someone like her. We have so much in common..." She laughed. For not being able to find the words, once she started, it didn't seem like she could quit.

Wearing identical shocked smiles, Jamie and Sue stared at Alex across the table. For their part, they were being good sports. Jamie found her voice first. "Have you told her yet?"

Alex couldn't figure out what Jamie was getting at. Had she rambled so much that she made no sense at all? "What are you talking about? Tell who what?"

Jamie shot a quick, knowing glance at Sue, for which she received a smug nod in return. She turned back to face Alex. "Have you told Jess that you love her yet?"

"*What?*" Alex gasped. Her head spun as if she had chugged down the entire bottle of wine. Of course she had been entertaining that thought herself. Over the past weeks, she felt

herself falling more and more for Jess. But for Jamie and Sue to also suggest that—was it that apparent?

Jamie and Sue again exchanged one of those silent looks that couples who had been together for a long time could—that look that says, "See, I told you so." They both began snickering.

"What?" Had she really fallen in love with Jess? The more she thought about it, the more she had to concede that that was indeed the case. But how did Jess feel? That was the twenty-thousand dollar question right there, wasn't it? Finally, she swallowed and lowered her eyes to the table. "Is it that obvious?"

Jamie reached out and gently patted her hand. "Sweetie, it couldn't be more obvious if you tattooed 'I love Jess' right across your forehead."

* * *

Jess dove into her workout at East Town Fitness Center with a ferocity that surprised even her. The weights clanked with each rep as she thrust the bar into the air again and again and again. She sucked in breath after searing breath while sweat rolled down her face. Her body was damp with sweat, gluing her back to the weight bench. But she didn't care.

"Are you okay, Jess?" Jordan leaned over top of her, spotting, deep lines of concern wrinkling her brow upside down in Jess's vision.

"Yeah, I'm fine. Why do you ask?" Jess panted between gritted teeth. She had asked her sister to come work out with her but from the look on Jordan's face, she was beginning to regret it. She knew that look well. It was Jordan's I'm-going-to-bug-you-until-you-tell-me-what's-wrong look and after today, she really wasn't in the mood for it.

"Oh, I don't know. Maybe since you're trying to kill yourself on the bench press, I thought there might be something going on. Call me crazy." Jordan gave her a wry smile as she helped guide the weight bar back into the cradle. She helped Jess sit up and tossed her a towel.

Jess dried the sweat from her face, avoiding Jordan's gaze. "It's nothing, nothing at all."

Jordan sat down beside her and threw an arm around her shoulders, pulling her close. "Say what you will, Jess, but whatever's going on is certainly not nothing."

What could she say to that? Jordan had her there. As much as she might want to deny it, Jordan was right—it was certainly not nothing. But what was it? Why was she so bothered by the confrontation with Terra? Terra had only been trying to protect her. And hadn't she apologized in the end? Of course she had. Then why was this bothering her so much? Or did it have anything to do with Terra at all? Finally, she blew out an exasperated breath, her shoulders slumping. "Fine, if you must know, Jordan, there *is* something going on but I'll be damned if I know what. I just feel like screaming."

"Then by all means, scream. You won't see me stopping you. Hell, I'll even join in."

Jess turned to Jordan and seeing her earnest look, had to laugh. If anyone would join in when she felt like rolling her head back and screaming, it would be Jordan. "You know, I believe you would."

"Damn right!" Jordan nodded her head firmly. She leaned closer. "So now that we've got that established, how about you tell me what's wrong? You never know, maybe I can help."

Jess sat thinking while Jordan waited patiently. When she finally opened her mouth, even she wasn't prepared for the words that poured out. "I don't know what to do, Jordan. I really don't. I feel like pulling my hair out. I jumped down Terra's throat at work when she badmouthed Alex, and for what—she was only trying to look out for me. I've never done that before. Terra's always been there for me. But it pissed me off so much to hear her knocking Alex. And to tell you the truth, I'm not really sure why I was so angry at Terra in the first place and that's pissing me off as well." Jess slumped over and tousled her short sweaty hair in frustration. She sat up, her chest heaving. "*That's* what's wrong."

"I see." Jordan stared at her, her eyes wide. "As long as it's nothing *big* or anything." She fixed Jess with a serious look.

Jess stared at Jordan for a long moment, then smiled. "Yeah, thank God it's nothing big, huh? What was I thinking? Silly me." She rolled her eyes.

"At least I got you to smile."

"You're always good for that, Jordan—my own personal stand-up comedian. Now if only you could help me figure out why everything in my life feels out-of-control."

Jordan tapped the side of her face with her finger, thinking. "Well, I've got an idea but I'm not sure you're going to like hearing it."

"Since when has that stopped you?" The words tumbled out before she could stop. She then winced. "Sorry, I didn't mean that. You're trying to be helpful and I'm throwing it back in your face. So, what is your idea?"

"Okay, but don't say I didn't warn you." Jordan smiled and cocked her head slightly to the side, not the least abashed. "You've become a bit of a control freak."

Jess opened her mouth to protest but Jordan silenced her with a finger.

"I'm not saying it's a bad thing. You've lost control over certain aspects of your life, and you're now fervently holding onto control where you can. Only makes sense."

Jess found herself nodding as she listened to Jordan. How could she deny it? That was her to a tee. Since she lost control of her legs, she would be damned if she lost control of anything else in her life.

Jordan leaned in, fixing Jess's gaze. "Sounds to me as if that's maybe what's going on—the entire blowup with Terra and everything—you're feeling a bit out-of-control."

"That's it right there. I feel there's a part of me that's out-of-control, as if I don't have any say-so in the matter. That's why I blew up at Terra today. It felt like she was telling me what I should or shouldn't do."

"Now this might come as a shock to you but I don't think it has anything to do with Terra either."

Jess felt as if she had been gut-punched. Not have something to do with Terra? What the hell. Hadn't Jordan heard a thing she had said? Of course it had everything to do with Terra. How could it not? "What?"

Jordan laughed and, with her arm around Jess's shoulders, pulled her in for a quick one-armed hug. "Told you it might shock you."

Jess finally found her voice. "What do you mean it's not about Terra? How can you say that?"

Jordan continued to smile. "Simple. It's not about Terra at all but *Alex*. I mean, it's pretty obvious."

Jess didn't know what to say. She shouldn't have invited Jordan to come work out with her. This was turning into a bigger fiasco than the scene at the bookstore earlier. "Obvious? What's obvious?"

"That you love her."

Her? Love Alex? What was Jordan talking about? Sure, she liked being around Alex. And it didn't seem like a minute went by that she wasn't thinking about her. But in love? Was that even possible?

"Look, Jess. I know how you feel about this. I know you don't think romance is for you. But don't you owe it to yourself—don't you owe it to Alex—to see where things might go? If you don't, believe me, you're going to regret it someday."

Jess sat staring down at her hands in her lap. It made a lot of sense. Maybe she did owe it to herself, maybe she did owe it to Alex, to see where things might go. She smiled. The idea certainly had its appeal. Why shouldn't she take her foot off the brakes, take a leap of faith, spread her wings—choose your metaphor—and see what might happen? What could be the harm in that? But just as quickly as her smile had come, it faded. There was no getting past the simple fact that she could never share intimacy equally with Alex and how would that be fair to either of them? Slowly, she turned to her sister. "I hear what you're saying, Jordan, I do. But there's no way that I can be with Alex, at least not like that."

"What you mean there's no way you can *be* with Alex? Aren't you *being* with her right now?"

"You know what I mean." Jess shot her sister a thanks-for-being-a-smartass look and wrinkled her nose.

Jordan took Jess's hand in hers and gave it a gentle squeeze. "Look, I know you're concerned about certain aspects of a relationship because of—how should I put it—limitations. But remember what Mom has always said. There's times in life where intimacy requires hand-holding more than anything else."

"I know but—"

"But nothing. Intimacy comes in all forms, Jess. Sure, maybe there will be certain things that you're unable to do. So what? There's a whole world of intimate things that I'm sure you *will* be able to do. It's not all about just one thing. It's not all about what happens below your waist. Have I ever told you what part of intimacy I enjoy the most with Tim?"

Jess cringed. "Ah, no. I don't think I need to know that."

"I think you do." Jordan crossed her arms, her eyes boring into Jess.

For a brief moment, Jess thought about sticking her fingers in her ears and humming loudly but she knew with Jordan, that wouldn't do any good. She would simply wait her out. "Fine, whatever."

"This may come as a shock to you but it has nothing to do with sex. My favorite intimate thing to do with Tim is to curl up naked in his arms, feeling his bare skin against mine, listening to some soft music while he feeds me orange slices. He knows how much I love oranges so this is the perfect way for him to share that connection with me and as you see, it has nothing to do with sex per se but everything to do with intimacy. Intimacy is what you make of it. It's not always physical, you know. Actually, I would daresay that most times it's more mental, emotional, spiritual than anything else. If you focus only on your limitations, on what you can't do, I guarantee you'll be let down, chair or no chair."

Jess found herself nodding as she listened to Jordan. When had her sister become so wise? What she was saying really made sense. She had never stopped to consider what things that could be termed intimate she was still able to do. She'd always focused on the physical aspect of lovemaking that because of her injuries,

she could no longer enjoy or at least she had always told herself that she could no longer enjoy. A lot of it probably came from her relative inexperience when it came to such things. She had only been with one person and once only, and that had been the day before her accident. So as much a she hated to admit it, her little sister in this case knew a lot more than she did. With that thought, she chuckled. "I just have to ask, when did you get so smart?"

Jordan shrugged. "I think it was sometime last Tuesday."

A quintessential Jordan answer. "You know what this means, don't you?"

Jordan raised her eyebrows. "What?"

"I won't be able to look my brother-in-law in the eye for months. Or eat an orange, thank you very much."

Jordan rolled her head back and let out a loud, rolling laugh. "Good. Then my job is done."

On the trip home, Jess kept playing her sister's words over and over in her head. Jordan might be on to something. And what had Jordan said—she was a bit of a control freak? She couldn't deny that. But maybe, just maybe, this is one of those situations that she didn't have to control. What had that gotten her so far—loneliness and isolation?

So what was standing in the way between them? The answer to that was simple—she was. If she were to be totally honest with herself, she had hidden behind her chair, used it as an excuse to avoid romance. And why? To avoid being hurt? No, nothing like that. She had avoided romance for the simple reason that she would have to give up some of her hard-fought sovereignty, and trust in someone else. But didn't people do that all the time, chair or no chair? Wasn't love supposed to be built on trust?

Jess felt her chest tighten. Love. That was ultimately what they were talking about here, wasn't it? So how did she feel about Alex? Did she love her? How could she even ask that question? She wasn't exactly sure of when or how or where but yes, she had fallen in love with Alex. Deeply, madly, tiptoeing through the tulips, head in the clouds, fallen in love with Alex. That being the case, there remained only one question—what was she going to do about it?

Without another thought, without time to talk herself out of it, she pulled into the closest parking lot, screeched to a halt, plucked her cell phone from the passenger seat and quickly punched in Alex's number.

* * *

Alex smiled as she saw the incoming call. "Hey Wheels, what a pleasant surprise." She had been rambling around her house all day, walking up and down the seemingly endless stairs. Since her conversation with Susan and Jamie the night before, she had been taking inventory of her apparently obvious feelings for Jess. But what next? Where did that leave them?

"Hey Legs, are you free?"

"*Why?*" She drew out the word.

"What do you say we get together?"

Alex felt her heart rate spike. "What do you have in mind?"

Jess paused on the other end. "Hmmm, tell you what. How about we order a pizza and crash?"

Alex found herself smiling even more. "Sounds like a plan!"

"Good. After today, I could use a quiet night in."

"Why? What happened?"

Jess simply chuckled. "Oh nothing. I'll tell you when you get here."

Alex grabbed her keys and dashed out the door. She hadn't been planning on seeing Jess tonight but it actually turned out to be a blessing. She had an idea that had been bouncing around her head that she wanted to share with Jess. This would be the next logical step.

Twenty-five minutes later, Alex walked through Jess's front door without knocking. Jess met her in the living room, skidding sideways on the hardwood floor with her chair, her hair dripping wet. "Wow, Legs, you made it in record time. I wasn't even ready yet."

"I didn't get you out of the shower, did I?"

"Almost. Five minutes earlier and you would have caught me naked."

Alex snapped her fingers. "Darn. Stupid traffic. I'll take any chance to see you naked. If only I had driven faster."

Jess rolled her head back and guffawed, the sound echoing off the ceiling. "Thanks Legs, I needed a good laugh."

"Why, what's up? Does it have something to do with what you said earlier about having a terrible day?"

"Oh, just Jordan being Jordan." Jess waved her hand dismissively beside her head. "She seems to have no purpose in life other than to nose into my love life."

"Oh *really*?" Alex raised her eyebrows. This was along the same lines as she was contemplating. Maybe tonight would be a good time to discuss her feelings. "And would I by chance be part of that?"

Jess wheeled over to the couch. "Of course, silly. Who else would there be?"

"Oh, I don't know. You're a real catch so there's probably a whole line waiting."

Jess rolled her eyes. "As if."

Alex sat down, plucking up all her courage. Finally, she looked up and met Jess's eyes. "Since we're on the subject, I've been thinking about putting my house up for sale."

Jess looked at her intently. "What's that got to do with my love life?"

With a bright smile, Alex continued. "You know how much I love being around you and hanging out. And these past few weeks, I've really grown close to you. Now don't get me wrong, I love coming here but I feel bad that you can't come to my house, not with steps everywhere. It only makes sense to find something more accessible."

Jess's glare hardened. "I thought you loved your house?"

"I did. I do." Alex swallowed, noting the coldness suddenly rising from Jess. "But this way you can come over to my house, maybe even spend the night."

"What the hell!" Jess suddenly exploded, wheeling through her living room so fast she was a blur. "First Jordan and now you. Why is everyone trying to run my life…"

"I'm—"

"...I don't believe this. I thought you of all people understood..."

"—sorry—"

"...I don't need..."

"—didn't mean—"

"...everyone telling me what I need. I'm not helpless you know. I can take care of myself..."

Alex tried cutting in. "I know you're not helpless. That's not what I was getting at."

"Really. It sure feels that way from where I'm *sitting*." Jess spit out the last word. "I think you should go."

"But...but..." All Alex could do was stammer.

Jess whirled around and pointed to the door. "Just leave!"

Alex hadn't seen Jess that angry since they had first met. She could understand completely what that had been about then, but now? What had she done? All she had said was she was thinking about selling her house. How had that caused this? She had thought Jess would have been thrilled. Weren't they becoming closer all the time? It seemed the logical next step. Or had she read everything wrongly? She stood slowly, Jess still staring daggers at her. "Maybe I should go."

"I think that's best."

At the door, Alex turned back. "I'll give you a call—"

"Whatever."

If smoke could have rolled out of Jess's nose, Alex had no doubt it would be doing that now. For the life of her, she couldn't figure out what she had done wrong. As the door closed behind her with an almighty bang, she still couldn't believe what had just happened. In a daze, she stumbled to her car. "What the hell!"

* * *

The echo of the door slamming hadn't even faded before Jess rolled her head back and screamed. "God dammit. Why does everyone keep trying to control my life?" Her throat rasped with the force of the words. She could understand Jordan—she

had always been the nosy little sister—but Alex? What the hell! Of anyone, she had thought Alex understood, especially after everything they had shared. But apparently not. And what was up with Alex wanting to sell her house? She didn't need that hanging over her head. This was exactly why romance wasn't for her. No one should have to change their life for her. That wasn't how relationships worked.

Jess wheeled around and thrust her hands against the hand rim, sending her flying through the living room. So much for pizza and a movie. So much for rest and relaxation. The only thing she felt like was screaming.

But as quickly as she started, she came to a screeching halt, looking at herself in the huge wall mirror separating the living room from the kitchen. The image staring back looked crazed, harried, out-of-control. She slowly ran her leather-clad hands through her hair, trying her best to flatten it down. As she stared at herself her shoulders slumped. What was she doing? Why had she attacked Alex—Alex who was only trying to be kind. Only wanting to be together with her. Maybe she didn't deserve Alex after all. Jess collapsed against her chair and beat her hands against the wheels. "Dammit."

* * *

Alex walked through the doors to the ER at quarter past eight. She hadn't been expecting to work on her night off but she had received a call only an hour ago. She was desperately needed since her good friend and colleague Johnathan Bryce had shown up in the ER as a patient instead of physician-in-charge.

At least it provided a distraction and she wouldn't have to sit home and rehash the blowup with Jess. She still wasn't sure what had happened. She had wanted to test the waters to see how Jess herself felt about her. And why not broach the subject by telling Jess she was thinking about selling her house so they could spent more time together at each of their places. No big deal, right? Apparently she had been wrong—very wrong. She could still hear Jess screaming at her. *Just leave!*

She felt her chest seize and she could barely breathe. What if Jess meant that permanently? What then? Would it destroy their friendship? She didn't think she could bear it if that happened. Jess had become such a large part of her life. There was nothing she could do about that at the moment, so her best bet was to push it from her mind and get to work. She grabbed Johnathan's chart and pulled back the curtain to his bed.

"John, it looks like you'll go to any lengths to get me to work for you."

John gave her a schoolboy grin and held up his right hand wrapped in a blood-soaked towel. "Wasn't exactly by choice, I can tell you."

Alex gently exposed the wound, a deep, gaping gash right across the meaty part of his hand, leaning in closer for a better look. The sight of John's hand made her wince. "I'm afraid to ask, John, but how on earth did *this* happen?"

"You're not going to believe this but…"

How many times had she heard those words in the ER? It seems like every other person through the doors said that. *You're not going to believe this, Doc, but…*Nothing surprised her anymore.

"…I was getting out of my car when I got to work when the Pyrex dish my dinner was in slipped out of my hand, and I tried to catch it before it hit the ground."

"Doesn't look like you made it, John."

"No. Worse part, my wife is going to skin me for breaking one of her best dishes."

Alex laughed. She had met Jessica on many occasions and knew nothing could be further from the truth. It was more than likely that John was dreading telling his wife simply because he didn't want to worry her. "From now on, I think you'd better stick with Tupperware, doctor's orders. I'll even write it up on a prescription pad so you can take it home to Jessica."

"Thanks Alex. Sorry I pulled you in on your night off."

"Don't give it another thought. I am where I'm supposed to be. Lucky for you, I do fantastic sutures. By the time I'm done, you'll barely have a scar."

"I knew there was a reason I wanted you to come in. I wanted to be treated by the best."

"Flatterer." Alex rolled her eyes. "I'll send in Maria to clean you up and then I'll be back to close up that hand."

An hour later, she finished up with the last suture—twelve in all, an impressive gash to be sure. John was going to be sore for quite some time but like she had promised, it looked good. She set aside the suture kit and leaned back to stretch, feeling the muscles along her spine cry out. "You know the drill. Take it easy, change the bandage in twenty-four hours and in two weeks take out the stitches."

"Thanks again, Alex, and sorry again about your night off."

"Don't worry about it, John. You'd do the same. We all have each other's back here." Alex clapped him on the back and left. What a way to start the night.

* * *

Jess pushed herself along in her racing wheelchair, her arms flexing, her muscles groaning with each thrust that propelled her forward. The wind was whipping through her hair. There was nothing better than a good hard run to clear her mind. At least that had been the thought. But as much as she tried, she couldn't get the scene with Alex out of her mind. Why had she exploded at the mention of Alex selling her house? It made little sense. Shouldn't that have been a good thing? Didn't that show that Alex was serious about what they had together? At least Alex had been until her little tirade.

Jess closed her eyes, the taste of bile in the back of her throat. She owed Alex an apology—there was no other way around it. As Jordan liked to say, she was going to have to put on her big girl panties and woman up. Maybe later, when she got home. Or tomorrow.

Jess pushed harder, her speed increasing. The wind whipping past her ears sounded like a hurricane. Her eyes watered from the wind. At least she was going to blame the tears on that. Deep dark shadows crawled across the trail. The sun had long set and

only the last glimmers of light from the quickly-purpling sky lit her way. A bright star peered through the branches overhead. Or was that Venus? She wasn't sure. She didn't usually stay out this late but she had completely lost track of time. Not surprising with all the crap bouncing around inside her head. The trail in front of her was completely clear, not another person in sight, which suited her just fine. She didn't want to be around anyone. Not the way she was feeling at the moment.

The hum of her wheels on the pavement was the only sound breaking the quiet night air. No birds, no frogs, no crickets, nothing. The silence was complete. However she barely paid any attention. The only thing that she could think about was Alex. She really hadn't deserved her wrath.

She didn't see the dark, fur-covered mass bust out of the undergrowth until it was too late. A cat, a raccoon, a small dog, she wasn't sure. She swerved wildly to the right, hoping upon hope to miss whatever it was. But just as her right wheel dropped off the side of the pavement, she tried correcting back to the left only to feel her chair unbalance and tip up, hanging at that impossible angle for what felt like minutes. It pitched over hard, snapping the safety strap and throwing her down the rock-strewn bank. She came to rest sprawled out across several broken up slabs from the concrete foundation of an old depot that had crumbled decades ago and been pushed over into the scrub far below.

"Shit." She lay there, panting. She could feel the stinging pain of multiple abrasions and the deep ache of numerous body bruises. That's what she got for not paying attention. When was she ever going to learn? Hadn't that been what landed her in her wheelchair in the first place—getting all wrapped up in her thoughts and not noticing danger until it was too late? No, that wasn't quite right. A drunk had put her in her wheelchair. She was responsible for this. She shouldn't have been out so late, going so fast, distracted. There was nothing else to do but pull herself back up the bank. Then she could hopefully right her chair, climb back on and get home where she would take a nice long soaking bath and try to forget about her horrendous behavior.

Jess dug her hand in behind her and tried to scoot herself back up the bank but something held her fast. She tried again with all her strength. Still she couldn't budge. She ran her hands down her legs, searching for whatever was holding her. She had barely moved her hand halfway down her left thigh when her fingers touched something warm, sticky. "What the hell?" Her heart begin to beat faster as she pawed around, trying her best to figure out what was going on, what was preventing her from moving. Just then, the clouds parted and the moon finally peeked out, casting a pale beam of light through the branches overhead. Jess's eyes grew wider and her chest tightened as she took in the twisted piece of rusty iron rod, used to reinforce the concrete, sticking right through her left leg. "*Oh shit!*"

CHAPTER TEN

"Help!" Jess called out into the darkness with no response. She really hadn't been expecting anything, as it was late. She patted around again for her cell phone, hoping that she had somehow missed it the first time but no such luck. Again she tried to pry her leg from the rebar that impaled it with no luck. "Damn it." She beat her fists against the hard ground. She was stuck there like a fish on a hook.

Taking a deep breath, she felt around the wound in her leg again. Even though she knew she was hurt, she couldn't feel anything. She slipped her fingers between her leg and the concrete, trying to grasp the full scope of her predicament, and pulled her hand back warm and sticky with blood. She stared at her hand in the pale light cast by the moon, her palm drenched a dark black. "Oh *shit!*" She knew that she was in serious trouble. Why, oh why, hadn't she stayed home! If she hadn't been such a bitch and chased off Alex, she could be home right now halfway through a pizza and watching a movie. Served her right in a way. Sometimes that karma could be a real bitch.

She couldn't very well stay there impaled like a frog on a poker so she again tried to lift her leg off the rebar. A fresh gush of blood poured from her leg. "You've *got* to be kidding me! Can it *possibly* get any worse?"

Not wanting to bleed to death, Jess peeled her shirt over her head for a makeshift tourniquet. She rolled the shirt up as tightly as she could and slipped it carefully under her thigh. She formed a knot and tied it with all her strength.

Perhaps the strangest thing about all of it was she couldn't feel anything. Her mind kept telling her that having a huge steel rod crammed through her thigh should hurt like a sonofabitch. Still, she felt nothing—no pain, no pressure, nothing except for the inability to move.

The moon had risen higher, bathing the entire area in a dim light. She could see her situation in greater detail. She had been right—she was bleeding heavily. The slab of concrete looked as if someone had dumped a gallon of dark paint over the surface. However, that wasn't nearly as bad as seeing her leg. The rebar wasn't just twisted but actually bent over. How the hell that happened was beyond her. So no matter how hard she tried, there was no way she'd be able to free herself without help.

Jess leaned back and stared up at the stars. How long had she been there? Not even ten minutes yet? By the look of the moon and the sky, it had to be close to eleven. That meant that barring a miracle, she could count on the early birds hitting the trail at what—six, seven in the morning? Why oh why had she stayed out so late?

All around her, the night came alive. She could hear crickets and a hundred different bugs chirping, twittering, clicking, buzzing all around her. And then things running through the underbrush. Raccoons? Cats? Dogs? Something else? Something much bigger? Hadn't she read that black bears had been seen in the area? Or how about coyotes? Would one of them try to make a snack of her? She jumped when an owl let out a loud hoot right overhead. *Hoot...hoot...hoot.* Her heart galloped. Did owls eat people, especially someone trapped and bleeding?

She was close to all-out panic. But she had to calm down and relax, get her heart rate under control. The faster her heart beat, the faster she would lose blood. How much had she already lost—a pint…two…*more*? How much blood could a person lose and still live? She wasn't sure but she figured it wasn't that much. By her calculations, she had probably a good seven or eight hours before someone might come along and find her. Plenty of time to bleed to death. It was so cold…

As carefully as she could so as not to jostle her impaled leg, she bent to inspect the wound. The bleeding had slowed to a seep. Good. Maybe, if she were lucky, *very lucky*, she might make it out of this. With that thought, she rolled back her head and called out to the deep dark night. "Help!"

* * *

"Hey, is everything all right?" Maria walked around the corner and stopped cold when she saw Alex sitting by the phone in the nurses' station. "Something's bothering you."

Alex looked up and tried her best to smile, failing miserably. "Yeah, it's no big deal." She shot a fleeting glance at the phone. "I was just trying to get hold of Jess."

Maria leaned over the counter, holding herself up on her crossed arms. "She's not home I take it?"

With a frown, Alex slowly shook her head. "I'm not sure. I usually call her when I'm on break whenever I work and we chat a bit. But I wasn't scheduled to work so…" Again, she shrugged.

"Maybe she doesn't realize it's you. I mean, it *is* late."

Alex glanced up at the clock. One in the morning. Maria was right—it was late. But she had called Jess many times this late or even later. Jess usually answered on the second ring, sounding wide awake. But not tonight. She had tried twice. Still, no answer. More than likely, Jess was ignoring her. Judging from her reaction earlier, she wasn't sure when or if Jess would answer the phone. Finally, she let out a sigh. "Yeah, I guess you're right. Maybe Jess went to bed early or something." Even as she said it, she didn't believe her own words.

Maria leaned in closer, her eyes narrowing. "Is everything okay between you two? You really seem off tonight. Did you and Jess have a fight or something?"

Alex let out a deep groan and flopped back in the chair. "I guess you could say that although I'll be damned if I know about what. Everything was going fine and then everything blew up. All I said was I was thinking about selling my house."

"Um huh." Maria leaned back, her arms crossed, a knowing look on her face.

"What? What's *that* look for?"

"And how did you put it to her? Did you simply say you're thinking about selling you house or what?"

"I don't know. I said something about growing closer to her, how much she means to me, and how it only seemed fair that I sell my house and get something more accessible so we can spend more time together."

"I see." Maria looked smugger.

Alex slumped against the chair. "What? What did I do wrong?"

"Where to start, Alex? Where to start?"

Alex pursed her lips and shot Maria a wry grin.

"First, you tell her how much she means to you. No big deal. But then you proceed to tell her you're going to sell your house so she can spend more time with you. That's a pretty big decision."

"I only said I was thinking about it."

"Alex, Alex." Maria sadly shook her head. "You should know better than that by now, girl. Women don't think like that. All Jess heard was you like her...blah, blah, blah...selling your house...blah, blah, blah...let's move in together."

"That's not what I was saying!"

"Maybe not but that's what Jess heard."

"Arggghh. This drives me nuts. It's like one moment she's fine and the next she pulls back again. Two steps forward, one step back."

Maria chuckled. "Honey, don't you know that's what you get for liking women? We're all a bit nuts. I don't think I could

do it. Being in a relationship with someone as moody and unpredictable as I am, I shudder to think."

"I see your point." Alex couldn't help but laugh with Maria. It was a good thing she had known her as long as she had so she knew when she was joking or not. "Still, I think Jess's leery because of her circumstance."

"I wouldn't doubt it, Alex. You've been in medicine long enough to know how people react. Sometimes it takes a lot to trust, especially after a major setback like a permanent disability. That changes the very nature of how someone views life and their place in it."

"You're right of course."

"Darn right. All I can say is Jess's really lucky to have someone like you. If anyone can empathize with what she's been through, it's you. Just give her some time."

Maria's words still bounced around Alex's head. *Jess's really lucky to have someone like you.* If anything, *she* was the one who felt lucky to have someone like Jess.

* * *

"*Heeeeelp!*" Jess's voice was now raw and raspy. She was freezing. It was probably stupid to keep calling for help. What was that saying?—insanity is repeating the same behavior over and over, expecting different results. Staying awake and alert was becoming more difficult. She wasn't sure but a little voice in the back of her head kept saying that under no circumstance could she fall asleep. Probably something she'd heard in a movie. Hopefully Hollywood wouldn't let her down.

She heard her cell phone ringing nearby, startling her. If she could only get to it. She was just about to give up when she spotted it glowing in the underbrush only a few feet away. Hallelujah, she was going to be saved! But as she stretched for it, her leg held her fast, the phone just out of reach.

"Oh come on!" Jess stretched again but no matter how hard she tried, her cell was nine or ten inches out of reach. Then her cell went silent and the screen dark. She hadn't realized

how much light the phone gave off until it didn't anymore. The hillside seemed darker than ever. She simply stared at the spot where her phone sat then let out a horrible scream of frustration.

"Son of a fucking bitch! Ten goddamn inches—is that too much to ask?"

She felt her heart sink. She had been so close, so close to rescue. Did someone up there hate her? Had she pissed off the fates somehow? Had she seriously wronged someone in a past life? Whatever it was, it wasn't fair. Finally, Jess collapsed against the concrete and shivered. She wrapped her arms around herself for all the good that did. All she had on her top now was her sports bra. Even though the night was warm and muggy—must be somewhere in the high seventies—chills still shook her body.

You're going into shock. She had a big twisted rusty bent steel rod shoved through her leg. Shock alone could be just as deadly as the accident itself.

Jess leaned back, listening for any sound of a potential rescue. Nothing. Not a peep. How long had she been there? Two hours? Three? She couldn't be sure. Maybe if she had paid more attention in astronomy, she could tell by the stars and the moon. However, judging from the phone call, it was probably twelve or one in the morning. That is if the caller had been Alex, calling on her break. And who else would it be at this hour? She had become quite accustomed to Alex calling late at night from work. It was a nice treat. But she hadn't thought Alex was working tonight. Hadn't she said it was her night off, which was why she had come around. Still, who else would be calling that late? Her luck, it was probably some stupid telemarketer who would have been no help to begin with.

Jess sat up slowly. There was no use in speculating on what might have been. She needed to focus on the here and now. She had to check out her leg. Carefully, she felt around the gaping wound. At least she was no longer gushing blood. It was more of a slow seep. But again, that phantom medical voice in the back of her head spoke up. It then dawned on her that the phantom voice was actually Alex's. Was she so far gone that she was now hallucinating? Or was it her base survival instincts taking over?

Whatever it was, the voice was insistent. *You need to loosen the tourniquet to get blood back to your leg.*

There was no use arguing. Besides, the voice had been right so far, hadn't it? Jess leaned forward and gradually loosened the T-shirt tourniquet. Blood oozed out. Lots of it. Whether it was the loss of blood or just the thought of it, Jess's vision doubled then faded. Her head spun and her stomach churned. She quickly yanked the knot tight again and collapsed against the concrete, gasping for breath. So much for her phantom voice. It just tried to kill her.

For some reason, that thought struck her as funny and she began to laugh, softly at first but quickly becoming more and more hysterical. Finally, after what must have been a good ten, fifteen minutes, she regained her composure.

"Thanks Alex." She wasn't sure why she blurted that out but it somehow seemed appropriate.

As if on cue, the voice spoke up again, sounding exactly like Alex. *You need to do that every hour or you'll lose your leg.*

Jess simply shrugged. Who was she to argue? "Whatever you say, babe."

* * *

Alex couldn't quite shake the nagging feeling that something was wrong. Since she hadn't been able to get hold of Jess, she couldn't push the thought aside. Surely, Jess would have calmed down by now, wouldn't she? Or was she still fuming? If she was, how long before she would take her call? She couldn't very well apologize if Jess didn't pick up the phone.

It didn't take much for Alex to imagine a hundred bad things. She kicked her feet up on the corner of the desk and leaned back with her hands behind her head, taking advantage of a rare lull in the emergency room, one of those precious moments when she could relax for a few minutes and clear her head. But as much as she tried to calm her thoughts, she couldn't stop thinking of Jess. Was Jess thinking about her as she was thinking about Jess? Or was she home, fast asleep, dreaming whatever dreams she dreamed.

"Hey Alex, you look like crap."

Alex looked up. "Thanks Maria. So subtle."

Completely unfazed, Maria flopped down in the chair beside her. "I'm just saying, maybe you should go home. We can get someone else to come in."

"No, I'll stick it out." As much as she might want to take Maria's advice, all she'd do is sit there and worry too. She had tried Jess's cell at least half a dozen times and even tried her landline more than once. Still nothing. If Jess wouldn't answer, she wouldn't answer. So, she might as well do something productive.

"Have you tried to get hold of Jess again?"

"Yes, but I've given up."

Maria reached out and lightly patted Alex on the arm. "Keep trying. What's the worst that could happen?"

"I don't know."

"Do it. Trust me you'll feel better." With that, Maria hopped up. "I've got to go."

Alex took a deep breath. Maria was right—she would feel better after talking to Jess so she grabbed the phone and quickly punched in Jess's number again. She listened as it rang. Once, twice, three times, four times…and her heart leaped when Jess's voice answered.

"Hey, this is Jess. Just leave…"

"Damn it!" Alex slammed the phone back down. For one second, one brief glorious second, she had thought that Jess had picked up but it was the same message she had listened to all night. As quickly as her heart had leaped, a sour hard lump settled in her stomach. Why wouldn't Jess answer? Was she still pissed or was it something else? Or did she even have her phone on her? Was it perhaps ringing and ringing at the empty bookstore with Jess home tucked in bed? Wouldn't that be ironic—here all this time she thought Jess was cold-shouldering her and it turned out she had left her cell somewhere. She hoped that was the case. If only that nagging feeling that something was terribly wrong would go away.

* * *

Jess wiped the back of her hand across her forehead. Her entire body was drenched in sweat, yet she was ice cold and shivering. She had been drifting in and out of consciousness. Every time she felt herself fading, that voice, Alex's voice, yelled at her.

Don't you dare fall asleep!

"I'm trying, believe me I'm trying."

If you fall asleep you'll die.

"I know…but I'm so tired." As time went on, it was increasingly difficult to keep her eyes open. And those words—*if you fall asleep you'll die*—she wasn't altogether sure she wasn't going to die whether she fell asleep or not.

An hour ago—or was it only minutes ago, she couldn't tell—she thought she had heard her phone ring again but she couldn't be sure if it was real or just wishful thinking. She kept hearing things moving through the brush, up on the trail, even coming down the bank. Every time, her heart leapt—she was about to be rescued—only to find out it had been a rabbit or a chipmunk or nothing at all. She couldn't be sure of anything anymore. Would she ever see the sun rise again? Sitting there in the suffocating darkness, it seemed unlikely. She felt not a sense of impending doom but one of almost peace. She could just close her eyes and drift off. It would be like going to sleep, no pain, no worry. And then…then…what? Nothing? Would she simply cease to be?

As she thought more and more about that, the brutal existentialism of it all, she was left with only one thought—what her family would think. Her parents would be obviously heartbroken. Jordan would devastated. But Tim would be there for her so that was good. Her friends at the bookstore would be upset. And Terra, oh God, Terra. They had never made up. How would she take it? Would she somehow blame herself? Knowing Terra, she probably would. And Alex…what about her? Well, Alex was strong. She'd be able to get over it.

Don't you dare give up!

"I don't think I can make it, Alex." Jess called out into the empty night, tears welling up in her eyes. "I don't think I'm strong enough."

You can, trust me. You're stronger than you think. Just hold on.

"For how long, Alex? For how long?" She was crying freely now.

For as long as it takes, hon. For as long as it takes.

Jess sat up, staring off into the darkness. The moon had completely set. Did that mean it was almost dawn? She wasn't sure. There was the saying that it was always darkest before the dawn. Or was it the storm? She laughed out loud, the sound ringing out into the night. That was a big difference whether it was darkest before the dawn or the storm. She knew which one Alex would say it was. If only she were there, she wouldn't be in this mess. If only she were together with Alex, maybe she could work up the courage to tell her how she felt. Her heart ached. Would she ever have the chance to tell Alex how she felt?

There'll be plenty of time for that later, Jess. Just focus on surviving.

Alex's voice in her head was firm, firmer than she'd ever heard before, almost like a slap. She wouldn't have been surprised if there was a handprint on her cheek. That voice left no doubt what she should do. She had to survive. And then? Well, that could come later.

With a renewed determination, Jess reached down to the makeshift tourniquet. Her leg above the knotted cloth was still warm to her fingers but her leg below was cold, clammy. Even though she couldn't see it, she knew the skin was pale. In other words, not good. Without blood, it was dying, which somehow struck her as funny. Here she was in danger of bleeding to death herself and she was worrying about her leg, her useless leg, dying. Still, she needed to loosen the tourniquet for a bit and let her leg get whatever circulation it could or she would lose it for sure. As she slipped the knot, releasing the tension, she could feel blood immediately ooze from the wound again. Almost as immediately, she tied it off again. Maybe it hadn't been such a good idea after all. If anything, the wound seemed

to be bleeding even faster. So if it were between her leg and her life, it really wasn't a choice.

It may have been more wishful thinking but as she glanced around, she could have sworn it was getting lighter. She was able to make out details in the trees and underbrush that only minutes ago she couldn't. Even the sky was no longer inky black full of starry pinpoints of light but a deep, deep purple, almost the color of a bruise. Could morning actually be just around the corner? Had she made it through the night? Or was this a hallucination brought on by exposure, shock and blood loss? Did she dare get her hopes up? As if to answer, she heard that voice again, the voice of calm, reason, hope, that voice of Alex's.

Just hold on a little longer. Help is on its way.

Jess collapsed back against the concrete, her head spinning, great blobs of darkness floating in her vision. If the voice was correct, if help was on its way, then dear God let it hurry. She opened her eyes and looked up at the tree branches overhead. She could just make out a light glow illuminating the scene. It *was* getting lighter. She could see more and more detail. The leaves in the trees above were green. She looked around her. The underbrush was also green filled with yellows and browns. As she stared, she felt her eyes begin to water. She had never seen anything so beautiful in her life.

She glanced down at her leg and immediately wished she hadn't. The red drenching her shirt tourniquet and the concrete was even more vivid than the surrounding foliage, almost psychedelically so. Her head spun more violently and she leaned over to dry heave. It was perhaps a blessing she hadn't had anything to eat in what, twelve hours? Maybe thirteen? It didn't matter. She wasn't hungry. But one thing her quick glance had told her—she was in bigger trouble than she had thought if the amount of blood lost was any indication. If she were to be rescued, it had better be sooner rather than later. With her eyes still closed, she leaned back and cupped her hands to her mouth.

"Help…"

Her own voice startled her. It was weak, raspy, tired. Worst of all, it was small. There was no other way to put it. Somehow,

its tenor seemed diminished, as if she herself were fading away. That alone scared her more than she had been scared all night. She couldn't give up. Not if there was a chance in hell of her getting out of this.

"Help…"

Again, weak, raspy, tired—small. She closed her eyes. *Please oh please let someone find me. Please oh please don't let me die here.* That was all she could think of.

Just then, as if hearing her thoughts, a scattering of gravel rattled down the embankment. She opened her eyes and twisted her head around. At first, she thought it must be another hallucination. Her mind was shutting down along with her body and it was her body's way of coping. But loose gravel rained down on her. Surely that wasn't a hallucination.

"Hey miss, are you all right?"

Jess could hear the voice just beside her ear but it wasn't until the owner of that voice gently laid his hand on her shoulder that it finally seemed real. With that touch her heart leapt and she began to cry. She looked into the face of her would-be savior, a young, short-cropped bearded guy in shorts and a Gold's Gym tank top. "Oh, thank God you're here. I've been here all night." She grabbed his hand tightly.

"It's okay, don't worry. I'm Rick and we'll get you out of here. Can you move?"

Jess almost laughed out loud. Move? She had been trying to move all night. Couldn't he see her leg? But before she could say something, he answered his own question.

"Oh dear God!" Rick gasped as he took in the bloody strip of shirt wrapped above the twisted piece of metal piercing her leg. "Hold still. Um…just hold still."

It wasn't like she had any choice. Still, she was simply elated to have someone there—anyone. "Not going anywhere." She tried to laugh but it sounded more like a dry, hacking cough instead.

Within minutes, people filled the clearing. Jess lay back, her arm covering her eyes. It was all she could do to stay awake. Her head was spinning and she couldn't stop shivering even though

the fresh morning sun beat down on her skin. She wanted nothing more than to go home, curl up in bed and sleep for at least a week.

"Miss, miss, can you hear me?" A new voice.

"Mmmmm." It was all she could manage.

"Don't worry. We'll get you out of here."

Jess faded in and out. She caught disjointed bits of conversation but nothing made sense. *Have to cut her out...Rebar completely through...Get the angle grinder...Must have just missed femoral artery...Miracle she's still...Stand back...Stand back...* Everything sounded as if it were coming from down some long tunnel, hollow, distant. Someone patted her face but she couldn't open her eyes. They were yelling at her, sounding frantic.

"Stay with me! Come on, stay with me! Don't you..."

But whatever they said next, she never heard as she drifted slowly, slowly off into nothing.

* * *

"Hey Alex, wake up." Maria tapped her on the arm.

Alex slowly lifted her head from the workstation and blinked. She had only closed her eyes for a moment and fallen asleep. Since the ER had finally calmed down around five, it wasn't a big deal. She could use a short nap. "What's up?" She stifled a yawn.

"Aero Med's on its way, ten minutes out."

Alex immediately sprang from the chair. If the Aero Med was involved, it was never good. "What are they bringing?"

"Female patient, late twenties, severe penetrating leg wound, blood loss, unresponsive. That's all I know at the moment."

Alex nodded, the adrenaline kicking in. She was no longer tired as she leaped into action. "All right, let's go."

Alex raced down the hall to the elevator, Maria at her side and Derrick the orderly taking up the rear. She jabbed the button for the roof, tapping her foot impatiently as she waited. When the elevator finally arrived, she dove in before the doors fully opened. With an injury like that, any delay could prove

deadly. Maria and Derrick piled in behind her. Within seconds, they were headed for the roof.

When the doors opened, they raced down the hall to the helipad. It felt like a hurricane with the helicopter coming in for a landing. Alex covered her ears, shutting out the deafening roar. The bright blue helicopter hovered, slowly drifting closer—fifty feet, thirty feet, ten feet. Finally, the helicopter touched down, blasting more wind than ever across the rooftop. The rotors cycled down, the ear-splitting roar starting to subside.

Alex waited until the helicopter door opened and then stooped, running toward the machine with Maria and Derrick at her side. The rotors still whirled overhead only feet above her. As unnerving as that was, her only concern was for the patient. She quickly climbed inside and looked down at the young woman strapped to the gurney, surrounded by two paramedics. Alex gasped, her heart seizing. It wasn't until Maria climbed up beside her that she finally found her voice. "Oh my God, it's Jess!"

CHAPTER ELEVEN

Alex stared down, unable to move. She no longer heard the helicopter roaring overhead. She no longer heard the paramedic shouting information. She no longer heard anything. The entire world had gone silent as she stared at Jess, lying motionless with bloody bandages wrapped around a large rusty steel rod sticking out of her thigh up near her groin, fluids running in, defibrillator paddles at her side. Her face was chalk white and her lips blue-tinged. She looked dead. But just as quickly as that preternatural quiet had fallen over the scene, the silence broke like an explosion. The helicopter roared, the wind from the blades like a tornado. Voices were shouting all around.

"…first liter of saline is in, number two…"

Another medic was talking directly to her. Alex snapped out of her stunned fugue. She wouldn't be any good to Jess if she fell apart.

"…she became unresponsive five minutes out…"

Alex quickly nodded. Her chest tightened at those words. Her mouth went dry. They needed to hurry. "Okay, let's go." She had a job to do. She needed to focus.

As Jess emerged from the helicopter strapped to the gurney, she looked even paler in the bright sunlight. Alex leaned in and glanced at the monitor, quickly assessing the situation. Jess's blood pressure was dangerously low. Her heartbeat was also high—not a good sign, but at least she had one. She pulled back the dressing, taking a closer look at the damage. The rebar had pierced directly through Jess's upper thigh. Alex swallowed hard. From the positioning of the rebar right by the femoral artery, it was a wonder Jess hadn't bled to death. Alex noticed the makeshift tourniquet. "Who did this?" She turned to the medic.

"She did it herself. She took her shirt and used it to stop the bleeding. Said she loosened it every half hour or so to let the circulation return. Probably saved her life."

"Smart girl." Alex nodded to herself and smiled. The EMT was right. That had probably saved Jess's life right there.

They bustled with the gurney across the roof to the doors. Once in the elevator, Alex further assessed the situation. Jess's radial pulse was weak. Not surprising. She had lost a lot of blood. She checked Jess's left foot. It was ice cold, the skin mottled a nasty bluish purple. Nothing. She tried again. Still nothing. "Did you get a pedal pulse?"

The medic leaned across the gurney. "Yeah, but it was very weak. It picked up with the tourniquet loosened but the bleeding started again as they were cutting her free so we haven't loosened it again."

Alex loosened the tourniquet. Blood began to seep in earnest. She quickly pressed her fingers to Jess's clammy lower leg but she wasn't feeling any pulse at all now. They'd need to restore circulation. Depending on how long the circulation to the limb had been compromised, they might not be able to save it. Also, the jostling to free her probably caused more damage to the vessels around that vital femoral artery. However, that was all secondary at the moment—Jess needed to be stabilized or her leg wouldn't matter at all.

The moment the elevator opened, they sped down the hall to the ER. A blur of people—nurses, patients, other doctors—

dove out of the way. They wheeled around the corner and into trauma room three, where everything accelerated more. Alex grabbed the corner of the sheet under Jess. Together they heaved her from the gurney to the ER bed. Even though Alex was only supporting a quarter of Jess's weight, she still was shocked at how light she seemed, as if Jess were even more fragile than she appeared.

Alex yelled out commands. "Call OR, have them get a room ready and get the vascular guys, respiratory and X-ray down here." She didn't address anyone in particular—they all knew their jobs and the phlebotomist was right there to collect blood. "Type and screen for transfusion and crossmatch four units."

"We're going to have to cut your clothes off now." Even though Jess couldn't hear, Maria told her what she was doing. Alex bent in close, quickly analyzing the situation. Within seconds, Jess lay on the bed completely naked. Although she had seen Jess naked, or mostly so, this was completely different. The woman lying in front of her only vaguely resembled the Jess she knew intimately. Her skin was bluish white, corpse-like. Even her lips were devoid of color. Nothing about the ghostly figure in front of her remotely compared to the vibrant woman she had grown so close to.

Maria covered Jess with a sheet and Alex snapped herself out of her thoughts. But as much as she tried, this wasn't just another patient—this was Jess. But she still had a job to do and for Jess's sake, she needed to do it to the absolute best of her ability. Alex checked her body temp—barely ninety-three degrees. It was a wonder Jess had survived the night. The girl was certainly a fighter. Alex turned to the ER tech. "Let's get some warming blankets in here. She's been stuck outside all night and she's hypothermic. Warm those fluids up."

Alex bent over Jess's injured leg, pulling the bandage back. The wound was grotesque—not only a puncture but also a nasty lateral tear. She loosened the tourniquet again. Blood immediately bubbled up, surprisingly forceful. "Whoa, let's get some pressure on that." Maria pressed a pressure dressing to the wound while Alex jumped back and quickly grabbed a length of

tubing to tie off the leg. "Must have just missed the superficial femoral artery. It's a wonder she didn't bleed out."

Maria nodded. "Lucky girl."

Luck didn't begin to cover it. If not for Jess's cool thinking and making a tourniquet, she would have died.

More people arrived. Voices called out as everyone did their jobs. They all operated as one—the sign of experience and professionalism.

Maria called out, an edge to her voice. "Her oxygen saturation is dropping."

Alex whipped around to the monitor. "Damn, where the hell's respiratory?" She quickly glanced out the door—no respiratory. She again looked at the monitor and Jess's oxygen had dropped further. "That's it, we can't wait. We'll intubate now." She swallowed, perhaps a reflex for what she was about to do to Jess.

Maria grabbed an intubation kit and quickly opened it, handing the endotracheal tube to Alex.

Alex leaned over Jess. "I'm going to have to intubate you, Jess. Just relax." Like Maria, Alex talked to Jess even though Jess couldn't hear. She stood behind her and gently tilted Jess's head back. Jess's lips were a shocking shade of blue that seemed to darken as she watched. As gently as she could, she opened Jess's mouth, held back her tongue and with the laryngoscope down Jess's small throat, she slid the endotracheal tube over Jess's teeth, and carefully through Jess's vocal cords. Although the entire process was swift, it felt as if it had taken an hour. "Okay, Jess, good job." Alex turned to Lindsay, a young nurse barely out of school. "Bag her."

Lindsay hooked the ET tube to an ambu bag, careful not to dislodge the tube until it could be secured. Alex listened for lung inflation, first on the right and then on the left of Jess's strong, muscular chest. Alex had her eyes glued to the monitor. Immediately the oxygen level rose. She looked back to Jess to see color returning to Jess's lips and face. "Okay, start another large-bore IV. Hang lactated Ringer's wide open—we need to get her pressure up. She's lost *a lot* of fluid."

As she said the words, she mentally kicked herself. She should know Jess's blood type. But they hadn't known each other that long and it didn't make for good date conversation. *So, what blood type are you? Why? Oh, no reason. Just wondering?* If anything could bring a date to a screeching halt, that would be it.

Like a well-oiled machine, her co-workers ran through their duties. Maria placed the second IV while Lindsay went to the blood bank. Moments later, she reappeared with two units and checked compatibility info with Maria. Everything checked out and Alex attached one unit to the IV and hung it. She watched the bright red liquid flow down the clear tube and into Jess.

Alex glanced up at the monitors. She didn't like the numbers. Jess's oxygen was still too low and her heart rate was starting to creep up. Then, without any warning, the monitor flatlined, setting off the alarms.

"…she's crashing, she's crashing…"

"Check the lines!"

"Lines are good—she's in v-fib."

"Dammit." Alex leapt to the side of Jess's bed and started chest compressions. *One, two, three, four…*"Push an amp of epinephrine." *Eleven, twelve, thirteen, fourteen…*"Get the crash cart in here, stat! Hit Code Blue!"

Maria wheeled the crash cart up to the bed and broke the lock, opened a drawer and pulled out two vials and syringes. She gripped the needle cover with her teeth, filled the syringe and injected the medication directly into the IV line.

Alex continued compressions. *Twenty-eight, twenty-nine, thirty.*

Lindsay, her face chalk white, squeezed the resuscitator.

"Charge the defib paddles to two hundred." Alex pushed down against Jess's chest, again counting in her head. *Five, six, seven, eight…*

In the background, the defibrillator whined as it charged. When it reached full charge, Maria yanked the paddles from the machine while Jen, another trauma nurse, stuck adhesive conductor pads to Jess's chest.

Alex stopped compressions so Maria could use the defibrillator. With a paddle in each hand, she aligned them on Jess's bare chest. "Clear!" Jess's body jerked, her back rising an inch off the table then she just lay there motionless.

The rhythm on the heart monitor bounced a couple of beats before returning to flatline. "Still in v-fib. No pulse."

Alex immediately began compressions again. "Push another amp of epi. Charge paddles again to two-fifty." Sweat ran down her forehead. "Come on Jess."

Again the defibrillator whined as it charged. Alex continued compressions. *Eleven, twelve, thirteen...please God, please. Don't take Jess.* She hadn't prayed since her family had dumped her in the religious nut farm. If God had gotten her into that mess then she had no use for Him. But at the moment, she'd take any help she could get. *Twenty-eight, twenty-nine, thirty...*

Lindsay squeezed the ambu bag. Maria again grabbed the paddles. "Ready."

Maria aligned the paddles on Jess's bare chest. "Clear." She hit the button. Jess again jerked. Alex watched her heart rate on the monitor, holding her breath. One beat, two beats, three beats...flatline.

"Dammit." Alex's heart fell as she watched the monitor. She resumed compressions. "Go with one milligram atropine."

Maria grabbed another vial, pulled out a syringe and injected the medication into Jess's IV line. "In."

Alex didn't look up. "Good. Charge the paddles again. Three hundred." The defibrillator whined.

"Ready."

This time Alex grabbed the paddles. "Clear." Jess jerked. She watched the monitor. *One beat, two beats...flatline.* "Shit!"

"Still v-fib...we're losing her..."

"No...we're not losing her. Charge again! Three-sixty."

The defibrillator whined. Alex took the paddles, pressed them to Jess's bare skin and hit the button. Jess jerked. "Come on, come on." One beat, two beats, three beats...flatline.

"Nothing."

"Charge again!" Alex resumed compressions. "Come on Jess. You're not dying on me." The defibrillator whined. People rushed about the room. Nothing seemed real. Alex grabbed the paddles yet again. "Clear." Jess jerked. *One beat…flatline.* "God dammit." Tears ran down Alex's face.

Maria placed her hand lightly on Alex's shoulder. "Maybe it's—"

"No!" Alex shrugged her hand off, still doing compressions. Her shoulders screamed in pain but she hardly noticed. "She's not gone. I won't let her."

"Alex…"

"She's not dying on my watch. Not tonight." Alex balled up her fist and slammed it down on Jess's sternum, hard, performing a precordial thump. Jess's body bounced under the blow. Pain shot up Alex's arm. She balled up her fist again and raised it even higher for a second shot.

"Wait, wait." Maria called out just as Alex was about to drop her fist. "We've got a rhythm."

Alex stopped her arm midair and stared at the bleeps on the monitor. One, two, three, four…nice and steady. Holding herself up by the edge of the bed, she finally let out her breath. *Oh thank you, God.* She couldn't believe how close she had come to losing Jess. Her entire body hurt from her throbbing hand to her aching back and shoulders. Her lungs burned as she drew in ragged breath after ragged breath. The only time she could remember being that exhausted was when she had crossed the finish line beside Jess during that 5K.

Jess wasn't out of the woods yet. She needed surgery as soon as possible to control the hemorrhage and get that chunk of rebar out. Jess may lose her leg. But as long as she didn't lose Jess, nothing else mattered. They could get through anything. She took another deep breath, still watching the heart monitor. Jess's heartbeat was getting stronger. "Is the OR ready? We need to get her in there now!"

Maria ran across the room and grabbed the phone off the wall. "They're ready whenever we can get her there."

Alex grabbed the side of the bed. "Okay, let's go."

* * *

Four floors later, Alex was met outside the operating room by Andre Romanokov, the head of surgery. A tall, dark-haired man with a strong Eastern European accent, Andre had worked with Alex on many occasions. "What have we got here?" The words were drawn and slow.

"Twenty-eight-year-old female paraplegic with penetrating leg wound. She crashed in the ER but she's stable now." Alex mentally crossed her fingers.

"I see." Andre lifted the temporary bandage and gave a quick peak at the rebar sticking out of Jess's leg. "You weren't kidding. How'd this happen?"

Alex shrugged—all she had energy for. "Apparently she fell out of her chair and somehow impaled herself on the rod." Her voice was weak, tired.

Andre clapped her on the back. "Don't worry—we fix."

As Andre turned away with his team to push Jess into the operating room, Alex caught him by the sleeve. "Take good care of her, Andre. She's someone special to…" Her voice broke.

With a wide smile, Andre nodded. "We'll get her back to you good as new. Promise."

Alex watched the doors swing shut behind Jess. With her fist pushed to her mouth, she leaned against the wall and slowly slid down until she sat on the floor, her knees tucked up to her chest. Maria sat beside her and threw an arm around her shoulder. "I'm sure she'll be fine." Her voice quavered.

Alex glanced up, fighting the tears that now threatened. "Oh Maria, I can't believe this happened. And after how I upset Jess yesterday. If she…if she…" She couldn't bring herself to finish the thought. She gulped. "I don't know what I'll do."

Maria pulled her in tight. "Now don't go beating yourself up over this. It's not your fault."

"I know but…" Alex winced, the tears flowing freely. The emotional toll rushed over her. She began to shake. "I should never have left her last night."

"Hon, that may not have changed anything. If this hadn't happened last night then maybe next week...or next year. Or maybe never at all. You can't go blaming yourself. Sometimes shit just happens. That's life. You've done everything you can. Now, you just have to wait and have faith."

Alex tucked her head down on her arms wrapped around her knees. Maria was right. Sometimes shit did just happen. Look at what had happened to her—thrown away by her own family. Look what had happened to Jess—hit by a beered-up redneck in a truck. Sometimes shit *did* just happen but that didn't make it any easier. Finally, she lifted her head and quickly wiped her damp cheeks.

Maria gave her one last firm hug and stood. "I've got to get back to the ER but I'll stop up later and see how everything's going."

"I should probably—" Alex heaved herself up.

"You stay here, sugar. That's where you need to be." Maria flashed her a wide smile. "Johnathan's coming in even with his bandaged-up hand and Tom's already there so we've got everything under control in the ER. You need to be here."

Alex slowly nodded her head once. "Thanks." Although going back to work would distract her, she was in no shape to see patients. She didn't need a malpractice suit on top of everything else because her head wasn't on her job.

As Maria disappeared down the hall, Alex leaned her head back against the wall and stared up at the ceiling. Every nerve in her body zinged with energy while at the same time she felt as if she could lie down on the cold linoleum floor right there in the middle of the corridor, close her eyes and fall asleep. Unable to sit still, she sprang to her feet and began pacing up the hall. When she reached the end, she turned about and retraced her steps. She needed to do something—anything—but this was all she could do at the moment. Back and forth. Back and forth. The clock on the wall refused to move.

If only she could have gone into the OR with Jess. She didn't know what she could have done other than get in the way. Still, she would have liked to know what was going on. How long

had it been? Twenty minutes? Thirty? How long did it take to remove a chunk of rebar from a leg? Surely not that long. But from the amount of damage she had seen in the ER, the real challenge would be repairing the torn blood vessels. That could take a while.

Alex made another pass up the hall then suddenly came to a halt. She'd been so focused on Jess, she hadn't thought about anyone else. Had anyone informed Jess's family? Would the police have gone to Jess's parents or her sister? If they had gone to Jess's house, no one would have been home there. So, how else would they know? Alex pulled her cell from her pocket and stepped into the thankfully empty waiting room where she took a deep breath and dialed Jess's sister Jordan.

On the third ring, Jordan picked up sounding as bubbly as ever. "Alex! What a surprise."

Alex again swallowed, trying her best to force the hard ball in her throat down. "Um…Jordan…I don't know how to really say this but…there's been an accident."

"Oh dear God…Jess."

Alex quickly relayed the basics to Jordan. "…she's in the OR right now…not sure how much longer."

"Okay, we'll be there as soon as we can." Jordan paused. "Hey and Alex, just be there for Jess."

That she didn't need telling twice. "Believe me, I'm not going anywhere."

* * *

Alex sat in the waiting room, drumming her fingers on her thigh. Over two and a half hours and still no word. She knew that a procedure such as this would take time but as someone waiting, it was torture. Jess's family still hadn't shown up yet. She had figured they'd be there long before but something must have come up. She cringed at that thought. Hopefully nothing bad. Over the years in the ER she had seen a lot of bad stuff so it didn't take a whole lot of imagination to envision what could

go wrong. A car accident while racing to the hospital. A heart attack. A stroke. She had seen it all.

Running all that through her head, Alex continued to drum her fingers, the pace steadily increasing. At the first sign of movement in the door, Alex sprang from her seat. Esther, an OR nurse Alex had worked with on occasion, bustled in, a surgical mask still tied around her neck.

"Alex, I was told you were out here. Is the family here yet?"

"No, how's Jess?" She didn't have time for pleasantries.

Esther took a deep breath, running her fingers through her short, gray-streaked hair and gestured to the chairs. They both sat, Esther placing a gentle hand over Alex's. "It was a bit rough—your girlfriend suffered a seizure shortly into the operation."

Alex gasped, quickly covering her mouth. A seizure on top of everything. "Oh my God."

"I know that sounds bad but we got her quickly stabilized. Doc was able to remove the rod and repair the damage to the artery. He's closing up right now but there shouldn't be any lasting effects. But as you know, she's a long way from being out of the woods. Our biggest concern now is vascularity to the leg, as well as infection."

Alex simply nodded. Infection would be a huge risk. She shivered as she pictured the contaminants covering that rusty, filthy chunk of iron jammed through Jess's leg.

"She'll be in a medically-induced coma, especially after the seizure and the cardiac events in the ER. Hopefully, that will help her heal faster."

Alex swallowed. How many times had she given news to a patient's loved ones? A hundred? A thousand? But hearing it from this perspective, it was different—*much* different. "So, how long until Jess's in recovery?"

Esther smiled. "Should be in just a few and Doc will be out to talk to you also."

As if summoned by her words, Andre popped through the door. Seeing Alex, he crossed the room in three large steps and gave her a somber smile. "Good news. Jess is now in recovery."

Alex let out a breath, sinking into the chair. "Oh thank God."

"As I'm sure Esther has told you, we're not in the clear yet but everything looks good. The next thirty-six to forty-eight hours will be crucial but I am confident she'll make a full recovery."

"Thanks Andre."

Andre's smile brightened. "That's what we do, Alex."

Alex nodded, fighting tears.

"Is the family around? I should probably fill them in as well."

"They're not here yet." Alex glanced up at the clock on the wall. Where were they? "They should have been here by now."

"No matter. When they get here, page me and I can fill them in or you can if you want."

"I'll do it."

"Good. If anything changes, I'll let you know but your girlfriend should be transferred to ICU in another half hour or so. You can go down there and wait if you want."

"Thanks, I think I will." Again the lump in her throat, this time a tear spilling down her cheek. Alex stood with Esther. Her legs trembled as if she had run a race and she thought of the 5K run. She had no doubt Jess would find that amusing. *Overdid it a bit didn't you, Legs?* In this case, she had no complaints. She didn't care if her legs completely gave out and she had to drag herself by her arms to the ICU, she was going to stay with Jess at all costs.

* * *

With a crash of the door, Jess's family came rushing into the ICU waiting room. Alex opened her eyes. She had been resting as best she could considering she had been up going on thirty-six hours but couldn't fall asleep if her life depended on it. She stood slowly, every muscle in her body aching.

Jordan ran to her, the rest of the family trailing close behind. "How's Jess? Where's she at? What happened?"

Alex took a deep breath. "Jess is still in recovery. She should be moved into ICU any time now."

Linda wrapped an arm around Jordan. Tim held her from the opposite side. Pete stood directly behind everyone, looking

as if he were ready to catch them all if they should fall. He leaned forward. "How did this happen?"

Alex slowly shook her head. "I don't know. From what I gather, Jess crashed her chair on the trail sometime last night. She was trapped all night and lost a lot of blood."

Jordan spoke again, looking more crazed than before. "What, you don't know? Didn't she tell you when she came in?"

Alex took a moment and gestured to the chairs. This was going to be hard. Once the family was sitting, she kneeled in front of them. "Jess, didn't tell me anything—"

Jordan cut her off, her voice rising higher in pitch. "Why not?"

Pete placed a comforting hand on her knee. "Jordan, let Alex talk. I'm sure she'll tell us everything."

"I'm…" Jordan swallowed. "Sorry…didn't mean…"

Alex tried to smile, relying on years of training but still feeling the fakery on her lips. "That's okay. I'll try to tell you all I know. When Jess arrived, she was unresponsive. She had lost a lot of blood. While we were stabilizing her, she went into cardiac arrest."

Linda sucked in a quick breath, covering her mouth. "Oh my God."

Jordan looked as if she had been slapped. "Her *heart* stopped?"

Pete, although appearing so strong before, slumped in his chair.

As hard as it was for Alex to relay this information, it had to be much harder to hear it. "I'm afraid so. We were finally able to resuscitate her but she had a seizure while in surgery. Jess has been placed in a medically-induced coma."

Tim leaned forward, his voice not much more than a whisper. "Is she…is she going to make it, Alex?"

As much as she wanted to tell them that everything would be fine, that Jess was going to pop out of this no problems at all, she couldn't give them false hope. Finally, she shook her head. "I don't know. She's in pretty rough shape. She's out of surgery but now we have to worry about the blood supply to her leg and infection. That piece of rusty rebar did a lot of damage. It was in

her leg a long time and she spent all night out in the elements. I won't lie to you, the next few days are going to be crucial."

Linda reached out and took Alex's hand in hers. She pulled her in close and dried the tears on Alex's cheeks. She hadn't realized she had been crying. But Linda dabbed away the wetness and hugged her as only a mother can. "Thank you for being there for her, Alex. I don't know what we would have done without you."

Alex tried to pull back but Linda held her tight. She didn't deserve such praise. It had been dumb luck that she had been in the ER when Jess came in. If it hadn't been for John cutting his hand, she would have been home. And if she hadn't upset Jess in the first place, she would have been with her and none of this would have happened.

Just as she was about to tell Linda that, a nurse appeared in the door. "You must be Jess's family. I just wanted to let you know that she is now in ICU and you can see her one by one."

As one, Jess's family sprang from their seats. Alex found herself being ushered along with them but when they finally reached the door to Jess's room, she held back. "It should only be family."

Linda grabbed her hand and yanked her into the room. "What are you talking about? You *are* family."

CHAPTER TWELVE

Her head bent and resting against the bed, Alex sat beside Jess. The family had finally left for some rest, what she should be doing herself but she couldn't bring herself to leave. Jess had spent last night alone, nearly bleeding to death. She wouldn't abandon her, not now. In the dim light, machines beeped, huffed and whirled. She knew what each and every sound meant but right now, she wasn't a doctor—she was a friend, a girlfriend, waiting at the bedside of the woman she loved. The respirator wheezed in and out. Alex reached forward, placing her hand on Jess's chest, feeling it rise and fall to the rhythm of the machine. With her head beside Jess, Alex closed her eyes.

She hadn't prayed since her parents had dumped her off at that religious asylum. Where had God been then? He certainly didn't come rushing to her rescue. And if that was what a kind, loving God allowed—no, scratch that—what, according to her father, he demanded, then she had no place for that in her life. And for the most part, she had been happy living her life without the constant condemnation and guilt piled on from her childhood. But now, she had nowhere else to turn.

With her eyes closed, she felt the soft *thump, thump* of Jess's heart pulsating against her palm. She took a deep breath. "Please God, I know it's been a long time and we haven't really seen eye-to-eye but I don't know what else to do. I'm praying for Jess because she can't pray for herself. I'm not sure she's going to make it this time. I've done everything I can. You and I might not be close but I know Jess believes and trusts so please, I beg of you, heal Jess—not for me but for her. I know we're not supposed to bargain—that's not how it works—but I'll do anything, *anything*, if only you pull her through this." Her voice finally cracked. "I guess…Amen."

When she lifted her head, Jess's sheet was wet. She hadn't realized she had been crying. All day she had been trying to hold it together, but she had no more strength. All her reserves were gone. The only thing left was raw, visceral emotion and as she sat there in the dim room, tears poured down her cheeks. "Please Jess, get better."

Alex looked up at the sliding door slowly opening. Maria stepped quietly into the room. "Hey Alex, how're you holding up, kid?"

Such a simple question yet she felt a fresh batch of tears. Alex wiped her eyes and tried to smile. "I'm hanging in there. I thought you'd have gone home by now."

Maria pulled a chair up close. "Been home and back. I've been on since seven but thought I'd better stop in to see how everything's going."

"Has it been that long? Good God. It doesn't seem like it." Alex laughed, a quiet hollow sound. "Then again, it feels like it's been a lifetime since Jess arrived on that helicopter."

Maria threw an arm around Alex's shoulders. "I'm surprised you haven't collapsed yourself yet."

"I tell you, Maria, I don't think I'm far from it."

"Maybe you should go home, get some rest. You know, try to forget about it for a while."

"No!" Alex violently shook her head. At Maria's shocked look, she took a breath and calmed down. "Sorry. I didn't mean to jump on you like that. I mean, I'm not going anywhere. I'm

staying right here beside Jess. No one's making me go anywhere until she's out of danger." Her heart thundered as she spoke. No one, no force in heaven or earth was going to make her leave until she knew for certain that Jess was going to be all right.

Completely unfazed, Maria simply waved her off. "I totally understand. Wouldn't have expected anything less from you." She nodded to Jess. "So, how's she doing anyway?"

Alex let out a long breath. After explaining in depth to Jess's family what had happened and the prognosis, she had hoped she wouldn't have to go through that again. Wishful thinking. Everyone who stopped in would want to know and it was down to her to fill them in. She braced her weary self and explained it all to Maria. Somehow voicing her fears made it that much worse. Jess might not make it. Softly, she started crying again.

Maria pulled her in tight. "Don't give up. That girl of yours must be a fighter to get this far. If she's anything like you, I know she'll whip this."

Alex tried to regain composure. She hadn't cried this much since she had been a little girl. But she couldn't keep falling to pieces. She needed to be strong for Jess. Alex pulled back, brushed her tears from her cheeks and tried her best to smile. "Thanks Maria. I'm sure Jess can use all the positive thoughts she can get."

"Not a problem. Not a problem. I'll keep you both in my prayers," said Maria as she stood. "Hey, I've got to get back but you hang in there, kid, you hear me?"

Long after Maria had left, Alex continued to hold Jess's hand, gently stroking it with her thumb, closing her eyes and drifting off.

* * *

At the door banging, Alex woke with a start. She quickly blinked, regaining her bearings.

"Sorry." Deb, the ICU charge nurse, winced as Alex turned around. "Didn't mean to make so much noise. Just checking vitals."

Alex yawned. "Don't worry about it. What time is it anyway?"

"Eight in the morning. You've slept here all night."

"*Eight o'clock?*" Alex gasped as she stretched her back. Although it felt as if only minutes had passed since she had nodded off, her back and aching muscles were telling a different story.

"Yep. I thought about bringing in another bed for you but you were so out of it." Deb smiled, the first smile Alex had seen since Jess had landed in the ER.

Alex found herself returning Deb's warmth and caring with her own smile. They really were like a family at the hospital. She felt her eyes burn. Quickly turning back to Jess to regain her composure, she pushed away her tears. "How's she doing?" Her voice shaking, she nodded to Jess.

Deb laid a hand on Alex's shoulder. "She's holding her own. Vitals are all good. Her temp's higher than I'd like to see but the antibiotics should get that under control. All in all, she's doing pretty well. That girl's a fighter let me tell you."

"That she is, Deb. That she is." Alex laughed, feeling a weight lift slightly. The image of Jess pushing herself to the absolute limit in a race just to prove a point popped into her head. Jess's determination, strength and sheer will had become one of the things that Alex loved most about her. She had no doubt that they would get Jess through this. Alex stroked the side of Jess's face with her fingertips.

Even two hours later as her stomach growled, Alex refused to leave Jess's side. It wasn't until Jordan popped through the door that Alex let go of Jess's hand. Jordan yanked her out of the chair and threw her arms tightly around her. "You've been here all night, haven't you?"

"Is it that obvious?" Alex tried her best to lighten the mood.

Jordan pursed her lips. "I know how you look at my sister. I wouldn't have expected anything less."

Not knowing how to respond, Alex merely shrugged. She wasn't doing anything that Jess herself wouldn't have done for her, even after their fight.

"So, how's she doing?" Jordan peered down at her sister with her arm still around Alex.

Alex took a deep breath and explained. Her stomach growled again, this time loud enough to be heard over the ventilator.

"When's the last time you ate?" Jordan pursed her lips, looking more like Jess by the second.

Alex thought. When *had* she last eaten? Not since the helicopter and that was now over twenty-four hours ago. Just that thought made her stomach turn and her head spin. Twenty-four hours—it felt as if a month had passed. "Honestly, I don't know."

"If you can't remember, it's been too long. How about we go get something in the cafeteria?"

Alex felt her chest seize. Leave Jess? No. Never. Not going to happen. She didn't care if she starved to death, she wasn't going to leave Jess's side. "I…"

"You don't want to leave her, do you?" Jordan smiled. "No problem. I'll go down and grab us something to eat and bring it back."

Jordan left Alex alone once again with Jess. She leaned in close, her lips nearly touching Jess's ear. "I know you can't hear me, babe, but I'm not going to leave you. Ever."

Jordan returned quickly, this time with the entire family in tow. Since there were so many, they took over a corner of the waiting room. Alex grudgingly left Jess's side but only because she could watch her from the waiting room directly across the hall. Tim helped carry food while Pete and Linda were eager for any information. Linda wrapped her arms around Alex. "Thank you so much for staying with Jess. You don't know how much it means to us to know that she's in such good hands."

Alex tried waving off the compliment. She wasn't doing anything special. And what was more, she didn't deserve any praise. If she hadn't upset Jess, this never would have happened. As she did her best to offer a smile to Linda, she pushed down the guilt bubbling up inside her. As she stared across the hall through the open door, she could see Jess, tubes and wires draped over her. Alex swallowed. Would there be a future together? If Jess recovered, would she want anything to do with her?

Finally, Jordan broke her train of thought. "Here, you need to eat before you end up in a hospital bed yourself." She thrust a tray with a large garden salad and a Greek yogurt into her hands.

Linda chimed in. "You'd better listen to Jordan. You don't want me to take you over my knee, do you?"

Pete let out a loud laugh. "She's not kidding either. She'll do it."

Whether it was physical, mental or emotional exhaustion—or a combination of the three—Alex felt fresh tears wetting her cheeks. She wasn't used to familial caring. As far as her family was concerned, she was going to burn in hell because she was gay.

Linda reached over and wiped away her tears and gave her a warm, sweet smile. "Everything's going to be all right. Don't you worry. And don't you dare forget, we're here for you too."

Jordan nudged her shoulder with hers. "You had better believe that, sis."

Alex swallowed. *Sis?* How was she to take that? She wasn't a part of the family. She wasn't Jordan's sister. Jordan's real sister had kicked her out of her house only two nights ago. If only they knew that, would they be saying all this? Again, she could feel the guilt coiling up inside of her. She shouldn't be the one being comforted. She should be the healer. She was a doctor. That was her job. But for some reason, Jess's family had taken her in as one of their own. With a thin, high voice, Alex could only squeak out a single word. "Thanks."

* * *

The afternoon quieted and Alex relaxed in the chair beside Jess's bed, staring at the ceiling. Jordan and the rest had gone to eat a little over an hour ago. Although she had been invited, she didn't want to leave Jess. No one seemed surprised. Andre popped in on his rounds to proclaim in his distinctly thick accent that Jess was a miracle. "Very good!" Alex couldn't agree more. She should probably try getting some sleep but whenever she closed her eyes, the only thing she could picture was the last

time she and Jess had been together. The scene played over and over in her mind.

At a soft knock on the door, Alex looked up. There standing in the doorway was the last person she wanted to see.

"You mind if I come in?" Terra waited with her shoulders slumped, her long white dreads hanging over her chest.

Alex braced herself. Nothing could be worse than Jess lying in a hospital bed, not even a row with Terra. "Sure, come on in." Alex's voice was weak.

Terra approached one slow step at a time. Finally, she stood over Jess, her back to Alex. "How is she?"

Alex shook her head. Terra couldn't bring herself to look at her. Fine. She had bigger things to worry about. "I won't lie to you, she's pretty rough."

"But she's alive."

That seemed like a strange observation but in her experience, people in shock said strange things. "Yes, she's alive."

"But she might not have been. Jess could have died."

Still, Terra wouldn't look at her but Alex didn't have the energy to care. "It was close."

Terra whirled around, dropped to her knees and threw her arms around Alex's neck. Alex froze.

"Thank you, Alex. You saved her. I know you did." Terra sputtered words through her tears.

"I'm not sure I'm to thank for that." Alex didn't know what else to say.

Terra pulled back and fixed her with her fiercest gaze. "I *am* sure. If not for you, Jess would have died. Jordan told me all about it, about everything you did, how Jess's heart stopped and you wouldn't give up. You're a hero."

She hadn't told Jordan or her family any of the details other than Jess had gone into cardiac arrest. She figured they didn't need to know how close it had been but apparently someone— and she had a good idea it was probably Maria—had told them what had happened in the ER. But she wasn't a hero. She was only doing her job. Just because it had happened to be the woman she loved didn't make a difference. She then corrected herself. Perhaps it had made a bit of a difference. Still at a loss

for words, she slowly dropped her head into her hands. "Terra, seriously, I'm not a hero. Please—"

"Whatever. You'll always be a hero to me and I'm really sorry for how I've acted. I was wrong about you." Terra fixed her with that gaze that said there's no point arguing. And even if she had wanted to, Alex simply didn't have the strength.

* * *

Alex passed the next two days in the same way. Jess's family showed up early in the morning and left late at night. Friends and co-workers popped in throughout the day. Alex still refused to leave. Maria brought her a pair of fresh scrubs and she was having her meals delivered by food service but other than that, nothing had changed. She still smiled and talked with each visitor, filling them in on the latest which was everything's the same and enduring more hugs and praise than she had ever received in her life. Yet with each compliment, each clap on the back, each teary-eyed thanks, she felt worse, the guilt burrowing deeper into her soul. Except for Maria, no one knew of the events the night before Jess's accident.

During the day, she could push those feelings aside. There was too much commotion, shared stories and commiseration to really have time to think. But at night, with only the machines working in the background, Alex had nothing but her thoughts for company. She had lost track of how many times she had silently asked for Jess's forgiveness. A dozen? A hundred? More? And whenever she wasn't pleading for forgiveness, she was praying for Jess's healing. "Dear God, I'll do anything, *anything*, just let Jess be okay."

By the time Jamie burst through the door toward the end of the third day, Alex looked appalling. She had deep, dark circles under her eyes and her hair was stringy and greasy. She had lost weight if the looseness of her scrubs was any indication.

"Oh my God, Alex. I just heard. How's Jess doing?" Without pausing, Jamie pulled up a chair.

Alex turned slowly and opened her eyes. She had been about to nod off in one of the few quiet moments. "Jamie, sorry I forgot to call you." Actually, she hadn't called anyone since Jordan.

"Hey, don't worry about that. I totally understand. You had other things worry about."

Jamie took Alex's hand in hers and squeezed. "How's she doing?"

Alex took a deep, labored breath, her throat raw. "Better. Her temp's down and they extubated her this morning so she's breathing on her own. Her leg seems to be maintaining its blood supply. All good signs but, she's still critical. Next day or so will really tell."

With her hands over her mouth, Jamie lowered her voice and leaned in. "Oh my God. I didn't know it was so serious. What happened?"

Alex was almost too tired to answer. She had relayed this story what felt like a thousand times but of anyone, Jamie deserved an answer. With another exhausted breath, she shared it all. But that deep, gnawing guilt burned inside her.

It wasn't until she had finished that Jamie took a close look at her, her brow wrinkling as she took in all of Alex. "So, how are you doing with all this? Forgive my saying this but you look like crap."

For some reason, Jamie's words struck her as funny. Looking like crap was the understatement of all understatements. Looking like crap would actually be an improvement. But no matter how bad she looked, it held nothing to how she felt. Unable to control herself, she laughed harder and harder, sounding more and more unhinged. Alex dissolved into hysterical sobbing. She had held it together for the most part. Now everything she had been feeling, fearing, dreading, hiding came pouring out.

Jamie slid out of her chair and pulled Alex to her feet, wrapping her arms tightly around her. Patting her on the back, Jamie rocked her back and forth as if comforting a child. Finally, Alex regained some control although tears still flowed freely down her cheeks. Jamie grabbed a wad of tissues from the counter and dabbed Alex's eyes. "Seriously, Alex, are you okay?"

A simple question. Was she okay? How was she to answer that? *Of course she wasn't okay.* She hadn't been okay since the accident. Strong maybe, okay no. Actually, she hadn't been okay even before Jess had been hurt, not since Jess had blown up at her and shouted for her to leave. But how could she tell Jamie that? She had been holding that secret in for the past three days. If she opened her mouth now, she had no idea what might come bursting out.

Jamie chuckled lightly as she stared at Alex. "What a stupid question. Of course you're not okay."

"No, it's fine. Really it is. It's just been a rough few days."

"I don't know what I'd do if Sue was lying there." Jamie shuddered. "I don't want to think about it. You've got every right to fall apart."

Alex found herself shaking her head. Jamie only knew half the story. What would she think if she knew everything, that in some ways it was her fault that Jess was lying there, fighting for her life?

"What? I know that look. Is there something else going on?" Jamie eyed her as if she could see right through her.

"Not really." Alex looked away as her voice cracked. She didn't believe herself. How was Jamie supposed to believe that?

"Oh, come on. I know you better than that." Jamie placed a hand on her hip. "There's something more going on. Now out with it."

Alex took a deep breath. If anyone wouldn't judge her, it was Jamie. "Actually, there *is* something else, something that no one else knows." Except for Maria, she added to herself.

Jamie leaned in, not saying a word, just giving a small nod for her to continue.

"It's partially my fault Jess was hurt." Alex's admission rang out hollow in the room. "Maybe more than partially."

Confusion warred with compassion on Jamie's face. After a long pause, she finally spoke, her voice soft. "Alex, what are you talking about? How can Jess's accident possibly be your fault, even partially your fault? It's not like you pushed her or something."

Alex lowered her head. This was proving more difficult than she had thought. She should have kept her mouth shut.

"You didn't, did you?" Jamie teased.

Alex looked up, her lips pursed. "Of course not."

"Then how could it have been your fault?"

Exasperated, Alex threw up her hands. "The night Jess was hurt, I was at her house…" She went on to share all the details cumulating with Jess demanding that she leave.

Jamie nodded throughout Alex's tale. "Let me get this straight, you got into a spat with Jess earlier that night and that somehow makes what happened your fault? I don't mean to sound insensitive but I don't see it."

Alex wanted to scream. Jamie wasn't getting it. She slammed her fists into her thighs. "What's not to see, Jamie? Tell me! If I hadn't said what I said, we would have spent the evening together. Jess wouldn't have been out on that trail that night, and certainly not by herself. She wouldn't have almost died, left to the elements to bleed to death alone. Everything that happened was because I had told Jess I wanted to sell my house and get one that would be easier for her to get around in."

"Whoa, whoa, whoa, Alex. This isn't your fault." Jamie grabbed Alex with a hand on each cheek and turned her face until their eyes met. "This *isn't* your fault."

"It certainly feels like it."

"Alex, you can't beat yourself up over this. Listen to me…" Jamie gave Alex a firm shake. "This. Is. Not. Your. Fault. Jess had an accident. That could have happened whether or not you talked about selling your house. That could have happened whether or not the two of you got into a tiff. Sometimes shit just happens. You didn't do anything wrong. It showed that you empathize with Jess's struggles. It means you're a great human being and friend who will put someone else's comfort before her own."

Alex shook her head. "Oh please, Jamie, trust me, I'm not all that. Really, I'm not. If it was that great a thing to do, then why did Jess blow up? Why'd she ask me to leave?"

Jamie chuckled knowingly. "Because that's Jess. Like you said, she's really sensitive about anything challenging her

independence. She has spent all of her adult life proving to herself and everyone around her that she doesn't need to rely on anyone else, even when that is exactly what she must do. What Jess doesn't understand is that *none* of us is completely one hundred percent independent. We all rely on each other every day. It may not be exactly PC to say it but Jess has been blinded a bit by her chair. Everything she sees or feels or experiences is first filtered through that."

Alex stood agog. Jamie made complete sense. The hard thing to believe was it was coming from Jamie. She had never pegged her best friend as the deep, inwardly-viewing type. She was always the go-full-tilt-save-the-planet I've-never-met-a-cause-I-didn't-like type. This was a whole new Jamie she was seeing. With a glimmer of a smile, she cocked her head to the side. "So, when did you get so smart?"

Jamie waved her off with a laugh. "I wouldn't say I've always been this smart. I've just hung around you for so long you've finally rubbed off on me."

Alex pulled her in tight. "Thanks. I think I needed this. Everything's just spinning around in my head at the moment and nothing is making sense."

"I know, sweetie. You're exhausted and this hasn't helped at all. I'd tell you to go home and get some sleep but I know how that'd go." She pursed her lips again and rolled her eyes at Alex. "How about we just worry about Jess getting better at the moment and there'll be time for everything else later?"

"You're right." Alex let out a deep breath. "Of course, you're right."

Long after Jamie had left, Alex leaned over Jess's bed, gently stroking her hand, her friend's words bouncing around her already overfull and overtaxed mind. *Worry about Jess getting better at the moment and there'll be time for everything else later.* Definitely easier said than done. But Jamie was correct—first things first, Jess had to get better. That was the top priority. Everything else could be dealt with later. Selling her house, upsetting Jess, having a fight—all that paled in the grand scheme of things.

CHAPTER THIRTEEN

Slowly, Jess opened her eyes, the light stabbing her retinas. Where was she? How did she get here? Everything seemed as if in slow motion. Sounds were far away, from some other room, from some other reality. Was she dead? Was this the afterlife? If it was, why was everything so fuzzy? She blinked her eyes. Even that effort felt too much. Her eyelids were like cement blocks. Each one must have weighed a hundred pounds. And her head, what about her head? Was it hollow? Or inside out? Did she even have a head? Of course she did or where else would her eyes be? They wouldn't be floating around all on their own. Would they?

She tried to speak but nothing came out. Her throat was dry. Then the thought hit her, if her throat was dry then she couldn't be dead or she wouldn't be able to feel that. Or would she? Nothing was making sense. Maybe this was hell. How fitting would that be? Trapped for all eternity as a pair of disembodied eyes and a dry throat. Surely, she hadn't been *that* bad in life. Before she could wrap what was laughingly her mind around

that, she tried to lift her arm. Something rose into her vision. It looked like her arm with a crap-ton of wires and tubes but it certainly didn't feel like her arm. She couldn't feel it at all. As if by its own accord, her arm drifted to her face where it met her dry, chapped lips. At the touch, she felt her lips with her fingertips, her fingertips with her lips, each second the sensation growing. Fingers, lips. Lips, fingers. Firm, soft. Soft, firm.

The room was slowly coming into focus. She was in a hospital. The experience when she was struck by the drunk in a truck told her that much. She was in a hospital so she at least wasn't dead. She tried to swallow. Nothing. Only desert dryness and what felt like gravel in her throat. She blinked again. This time at least her eyelids didn't feel as heavy. Progress. The sounds of the room were growing louder with every second—a general cacophony.

Jess moved her head, a monumental blunder. The room spun and her vision fuzzed to black. Okay, she wasn't going to try that again soon. Her stomach flopped around like an out-of-balance washer. If her throat wasn't so dry, she'd probably have thrown up. So at least that was good. She hated just lying there. She needed to do something. She needed to get up. She needed to get out of there. Her deeply competitive drive kicked in. She'd be damned if she let a little thing like lying in the hospital slow her down.

Keeping her eyes closed, she tried to lift her arm, this time the left. She didn't want to deal with all the tubes and wires on her right. But as hard as she tried, her arm wouldn't budge. It felt as if it were held down, pinned against the bed. She flexed her fingers—that didn't work either. She couldn't move her hand. Something held it tightly. Then she realized, her arm wasn't pinned down, her hand wasn't trapped. No, it wasn't anything like that. Someone was *holding* her hand.

With all the strength she could muster, Jess slowly turned her head and opened her eyes. There beside her, with her head lying on the side of the bed, was Alex. Alex, with her eyes closed, dark circles beneath each one, slept beside her, their fingers intertwined. Her hair was greasy and tousled every

which direction. Maybe it was the medications or her senses still hadn't come completely come back but Alex looked thinner, almost haggard. Then it hit Jess. How long had she been out? Hours? Days? Months? *More?* How much time had actually passed? How much had she missed?

A voice cried out, echoing painfully in her head.

"Jess! You're awake."

The voice was on her right side and in her shock, Jess whirled around. Big mistake. The room went black again. She felt herself slipping, much like Alice sliding down the rabbit hole. Then everything swam back into view. Jordan's face gradually came into focus, her hands clapped over her mouth. Jess collapsed back against the bed.

From her left, Alex gave her hand a gentle squeeze. "Welcome back, Wheels."

Alex's endearment made her want to smile if only she had the strength. Whipping her head around to see Jordan had sapped what little energy she had. Still, she worked her mouth, her lips slowly moving. Finally, with the feeling of sand packing her throat, she managed a very quiet grunt. "Wa…water." That was all she could do.

Alex jumped up. "Hold on. I'll get you something."

Jordan, also on her feet, darted for the door. "I'll get someone."

Seconds later, Alex helped Jess up in the bed and held a cup under her nose. Carefully, she directed the straw to Jess's parched lips. "Slowly now. Not too much or you'll be sick."

The water passed over her tongue and down her throat. Oh glorious cold wetness! Jess couldn't remember anything feeling so good. It was all she could do not to gulp, simply tip the cup up and pour it straight down her throat. If she had any strength in her arms, she would have done just that, but as it was, Alex pulled the cup back.

"Whoa, whoa, Jess. Take it slow. It's been a while since you've drunk anything. Give your body time to adjust."

She almost cried as Alex pulled the cup away. Her body screamed, more, more, more. But then it hit her, Alex's words.

It's been a while... She swallowed, this time her throat not as dry. "How long?"

Alex leaned in, her voice soft. "Five days."

Jess wrapped her mind around that. Five days. She had no point of reference. It could have been five weeks, five months, or five years. She could live with five days. "Wha...what..."

"Shhh." Alex pressed her finger to Jess's dry, chapped lips. "No more questions right now. There'll be plenty of time for that later. Just rest."

Jordan returned at a run with a middle-aged woman with short, spiky gray hair. She ran around the far side of the bed, looking as if she were about to hyperventilate. Jess smiled. Maybe Jordan was the one that needed to rest. If she were any more hyped up, she would probably explode.

Alex made way as the woman stepped up beside her. "This is Dr. Harris, Jess. She's your doctor in the ICU. She needs to check you."

"Hi Jess. You can call me Becky. None of this Dr. Harris stuff." She smiled over at Alex. "You've given us a good scare. How are you feeling?"

Jess nodded, a small, barely perceptible movement. "Okay, I guess."

Becky continued to check her over. "Well, you're looking good. Everything's right where I'd like to see them."

Jess licked her lips. "So, I'm going to live." Her voice was still thin, weak.

Becky let out a rolling laugh. "Hold on there. No self-diagnoses please." She pulled out her stethoscope and listened to Jess's heart and lungs then looked into her eyes with an ophthalmoscope.

Jess winced at the bright light. Instead of light, it felt as if the doc was shooting an arrow through her eye.

"Bright, I know." Becky peeked around the scope. "Sorry. But everything there looks good. Let's take a look at your leg— that was a pretty nasty wound."

Becky replaced the sheet, and stood back with a smile. "I think you're right—you're going to live. And keep that leg!"

Jess laughed and immediately regretted it as it turned into a dry, hacking cough. Her chest rasped and grated as if she had swallowed the world's largest dust kitty.

Becky gently placed her hand on Jess's chest. "Easy, easy. It's going to take a little time to get back to normal. Lots of work ahead of you, okay?"

Jess nodded. She didn't think she could exert herself if her life depended on it, which struck her as funny seeing as what she had recently been through.

"Okay, I'm going to leave you to rest." Becky patted Jess on the shoulder. "I'll be back in a bit later and see if we can get you up and moving. But for now, I want you to concentrate on getting those lungs back into gear. You and that leg of yours have been through a rough ordeal." She gave Jess a bright wink.

Jordan chimed in. "Don't worry, Doc, I'll make sure she behaves."

Jordan and Alex pulled up their chairs, one on each side. Jess leaned back against the bed, closing her eyes. After a long moment, she spoke, her voice growing stronger. "What all happened? All I remember is the emergency crew showing up and that was it until I woke up here. How bad was it?"

Alex and Jordan exchanged looks and Alex leaned in recounting everything. When she finished, Jess sat stunned.

"So, all and all, I've had a busy couple of days."

Jordan laughed and cried at the same time. "You have got to be shitting me, Jess. You almost die and all you have to say is '*I've had a busy couple of days.*' Here, we've all been worried sick this entire time. *I've had a busy couple of days.* Unbelievable!"

Jess smiled. Feeling her energy drain again, she fought to keep her eyes open. She turned from Jordan to Alex and winced at the sight of her. What had she been doing with herself? Alex looked worse than when she had collapsed after that benefit 5K. Whatever it was, she didn't have the strength to deal with it. "Alex, you need to go home."

Alex's eyes opened wide and she shook her head. "I'm not going anywhere. Not until I know you're better."

Jess sighed. The last thing she needed was to feel suffocated by Alex. She didn't have a choice with Jordan but she did with

Alex. "Really, you need to go. I'll be fine by myself. Better than fine."

Alex swallowed. "But…but…"

Jess tilted her head up and groaned. Alex didn't know when to back off. Certainly she appreciated her visiting while she was in the hospital—probably stopped by on her break—but she didn't need someone to hold her hand. She had gotten through this once, she could do it again. That was the entire reason she had been so pissed when Alex had offered to sell her house. She didn't need someone holding her hand as if she were a little child. "Look, Alex, you don't need to be here. I can do this just fine on my own. Now, go home, get some rest. You look like crap."

Alex stared opened-mouthed. "Ah…but—"

"Alex, just leave. Please."

Alex slowly nodded and walked out the door without a word.

Jordan stared down at Jess, her jaw muscles working. Jess could feel her eyes on her even before Jordan spoke. "What the hell was that?"

"What?" Jess bristled. She didn't need to get it from Jordan too.

"I can't believe you just did that. Is that how you treat people who care for you? If you weren't in that bed I'd—"

"You'd what? What exactly would you do, Jordan?"

Jordan let out a long, exasperated breath. "I'd show you some manners, some compassion, some empathy. I'll chalk it up to the meds but you don't seem to have any of that right now."

"I said please."

"Oh, come on. *I said please.* As if that made a difference. You should have seen Alex's face. She was devastated. And after everything's she's done for you. That's a fine how-do-you-do. Now if you'll excuse me, I'm going to see if I can catch Alex and…I don't know…apologize for your rudeness."

"Fine." Jess didn't open her eyes as Jordan stomped out of the room. How dare she lecture her on manners? She was the one lying in a bed, not her. Jordan was just like everyone else. When would they get it—she could manage on her own—at all costs.

* * *

Alex punched the elevator button for the lobby again, this time sending a stab of pain through her finger. "Come on, dammit." She couldn't get out of the hospital fast enough. How had things deteriorated with Jess so quickly? One second, all had been fine. The next, blammo. Totally out of left field. It was the selling-her-house incident all over again. All she wanted to do was show Jess that she cared. How could she do that when whenever she tried, Jess kicked her out? She must be doing something wrong but for the life of her, she didn't know what.

"Alex! Alex, wait up!"

At the sound of Jordan's call, her shoulders slumped. Just what she didn't need—round two, this time with Jess's sister. She punched the elevator button again—*please dear God open up you stupid ass elevator*—with no luck.

Jordan slid to a stop in front of her, gasping. "Hey, don't go yet. I'm sorry about Jess in there. You didn't deserve that. I don't know what's wrong with her. You'd think she'd be happy waking up and seeing you there. I mean, you've been at her side the entire time."

Not what she had been expecting, that was for sure. But somehow, it would have been easier if Jordan had been yelling at her. Jordan's words stabbed through her heart more painfully than if she had been bitching her out. She stared at Jordan, unable to think of a response. Tell her that this wasn't the first time this had happened? The first time had been the night Jess had been impaled and almost died? She couldn't lay that on Jordan, not after all the family's support.

Jordan dropped her hand on Alex's shoulder, giving her a gentle squeeze. "Look, I'm sure Jess didn't mean what she said. I don't know—maybe she was just shocked to see you there. Or maybe she was ashamed to be in a hospital bed. You know how she hates feeling like an invalid. Heaven forbid she needed someone else's help."

Alex nodded. She had to rely on a ton of others to save her life. But still, wasn't that what everyone had to do every day?

Alex could see the humor in it all. Who was she to criticize when it came to relying on others? She wasn't exactly the poster child for social interconnectedness. Finally, she found her voice and did her best to smile. "I hear what you're saying, Jordan. I do. But I don't think Jess wants me around. You heard her. Maybe it's best if I leave her be. She has bigger things to worry about at the moment. She's been unconscious. Maybe she'll feel better once her head settles."

Jordan shook her head in disagreement. "You love Jess, right? There's no sense denying it, I've seen how you are with her, how you look at her. I've seen you over the past few days. You love her."

Alex let out a deep sigh. Of course she loved Jess. She couldn't deny it. But was that enough? How could that make a difference if Jess didn't want her around? Nodding in acquiescence, she dried her eyes. "Yes, I love Jess."

Jordan threw her arms around Alex, drawing her into a fierce hug. She whispered into Alex's ear. "Then don't give up on my sister. *Please*. Just give her time. She'll come around. I'm sure of it."

Alex swallowed, fighting against more tears. "I'll try." It was all she could manage.

Jordan gave her one last rib-crushing squeeze before letting her go. "Good. For what it's worth, you're the best thing that's ever happened to her. I should know. I'm her little sister after all. We keep track of these things."

Alex managed a small smile. "Thanks, Jordan. I think Jess is pretty lucky to have you as a little sister too."

As Alex walked out the hospital's main doors, she could still hear Jordan's words ringing in her head. *Don't give up on my sister.* The last thing she wanted to do. She had told Jess, told herself, that she would always stand beside Jess at all costs. But how was she not to give up on Jess when Jess seemed to have given up on her?

* * *

"Hey, there's the miracle girl. So when did they move you to some new digs?" Terra popped through the door, her dreads flying.

Jess collapsed back against the bed and let out a sigh of relief. She had thought Terra had been her dear little sister coming back for another go at her. It had been two days since she had left ICU and in that time, Jordan had constantly nagged her about Alex. Alex this…Alex that…Alex, Alex, Alex. She was sick of hearing about Alex. She had actually began zoning out whenever Jordan talked about her or, pretending to fall asleep, although she wasn't so sure Jordan was buying the latter. "Thank God, it's you, Terra. Let me tell you, you're a sight for sore eyes. I'm about to go out of my head. Save me."

Terra plopped down on the edge of Jess's bed. "Why? What's up? Not enjoying the awesome hospital food or these cute nurses." She gave Jess a deeply salacious wink.

Jess burst out laughing. Leave it to Terra to take her mind off everything. "Jordan has been driving me insane. I don't know how many times I've had to tell her to cut it out. I swear they're going to have to move me to the psych ward soon."

"Jordan? What's up with her? I thought she was your number one supporter—besides me of course."

Jess rolled her eyes. "Usually she is. But ever since I woke up, she's been bugging the living hell out of me about Alex. She won't stop. I'm not sure how much more I can take."

Terra quickly glanced around the room. "Where is the good doc anyway? I'd have thought she'd be right here beside you."

"Oh God, not you too." Jess let out a long, low groan and slumped against the bed. "When is everyone going to leave me alone? Jesus, you'd think after all that's happened, there would be bigger things to worry about but *no!* Everyone's more concerned about Alex than anything else."

"Wow, where's *all* that coming from?" Terra stared in disbelief. "I was just asking where the good doc was?"

"Stop calling her that!"

Terra waved her hands in front of her. "Okay, okay. Alex then. Geez, Jess. Don't bite my head off. Believe it or not, I'm

here for you. We all are. So maybe try not to jump down my throat."

Seeing the look on Terra's face, Jess lowered her eyes to her hands in her lap and mumbled. "I didn't…you know…" She hadn't meant to attack her best friend but the entire situation with Alex was driving her nuts. She didn't need anyone running her life—not Terra, not Jordan and certainly not Alex.

"Hey, whatever's going on, you know you can talk to me about anything. Did something happen between you and the good…I mean Alex? I thought things were going great with you two."

"Ah…" What was she thinking? Terra would understand. She wasn't exactly Alex's greatest fan. "They were, I guess. But then Alex came over—this was the night I got hurt—and she says she's thinking about selling her house and getting something more accessible for me. Can you believe that? So I told her to leave. And then I wake up here in the hospital and she's right there again. I mean, I can understand Jordan being there but Alex? Talk about suffocating. So I told her to leave again."

Terra gaped at her. "What about me? What if I had been there? Would that have been all right? Or would you have wanted me to leave too?"

"Don't be silly. You're always welcome." Jess waved her off nonchalantly.

Terra's voice started to rise. "Then what is it with Alex? Why don't you want her here?"

Jess bristled again. This wasn't going how she had pictured. "I'll tell you why. I don't need someone holding my hand. Talk about being smothered. I—"

"I, I, I. That's all I'm hearing from you. Jesus Christ Jess, talk about being selfish. How about showing a bit of appreciation. It was Alex that saved your life after all."

Terra's words hit like a slap. She had never talked to her like that before. Terra had always been her supportive friend, willing to throw herself in front of trouble like a warrior princess. Hadn't it been Terra who had hated Alex from the beginning? Wasn't it her that had to convince Terra to give Alex a break?

But then Terra's words sunk in further. "Saved my life? What are you talking about?"

Terra grabbed her by both shoulders. "You died in the ER. Your heart stopped. And it was Alex who wouldn't give up. She never stopped. I heard from the nurse who was there, everyone thought you were gone. But Alex wouldn't accept that."

"But, but, but..." None of that made any sense. "Jordan didn't say anything about that. Neither did Mom and Dad. Just that I crashed in the ER. Are you sure?"

"Damn right I'm sure. You're sitting there right now, able to bitch about Alex smothering you because she wouldn't give up on you when everyone else had. She. Saved. Your. Life. And I'll tell you another thing—" Terra jabbed Jess in the chest with her finger "—Alex never once left your side. She stayed here the entire time, day and night. She wouldn't leave until she knew you were all right. So, what do you have to say to that?"

Jess felt her head spinning. Alex wouldn't give up on her. Alex saved her life. And how did she thank her? She kicked her out of the room. Why hadn't Jordan or her parents said something? Or had they and she hadn't been listening? Her stomach lurched. The bitter taste of bile rose in the back of her throat. "But...but...I don't need my hand held." Her voice pleading, barely a squeak.

Terra patted her on the shoulder. "Sweetie, we all need someone to hold our hand once in a while."

Jess closed her eyes and let out a long sigh. "I've been such a bitch."

"Yes, you have." Terra wore a deeply wry grin.

"Gee, Terra, thanks for taking my side. When did you start sticking up for Alex? I thought you didn't care for her."

"Since she saved your life and asked nothing more than to sit at your side until you were okay. I was wrong about her. Dead wrong."

And apparently so was she. Alex had never asked anything in return. She had simply offered her friendship, her love, her heart. And how had she repaid it? By acting like a spoiled teenaged brat. With that thought, she cringed. "Oh God, what am I going to do now?"

Terra laughed. "It's obvious how she feels about you and whether or not you want to admit it, I know how you feel about her. What did Alex do when you first met? Remember that? It didn't go so well either. What was that you said?"

"What a bitch." Jess groaned, remembering all too well their first meeting and she knew too what had to be done. "I'm going to have to swallow my pride and apologize, aren't I?"

"Damn straight. This time you're the bitch. So you're going to have to own up to it just like Alex did."

"Great. And how am I supposed to do that? Jordan hasn't brought my chair in yet—I think she's deliberately forgetting it—payback for me not listening to her. She probably thinks that if I had my chair, I'd try to escape, which is exactly what I would do. So I'm stuck here at the mercy of the nurses and whatever chair they bring me. Even if I did know where Alex is, I have no way to get there and I highly doubt she'd come here after what I've done."

Terra sprang to her feet. "Wait here. I've got an idea." And with that, she tore from the room.

Jess cupped her hand to her mouth and called out as Terra disappeared. "It's not like I'm going anywhere."

A couple of minutes later, Terra popped back in, this time wearing a set of scrubs and pushing a wheelchair.

"What the—"

"Shhhh." Terra glanced over her shoulder as if checking for witnesses. "This is a black ops. Completely hush-hush."

"What are you doing? And where did you get those scrubs?"

Terra wheeled the chair up to her bed. "Ask me no questions and I'll tell you no lies. Now come on, let's get you in this chair before we get caught."

Jess shook her head as she scooted to the edge of the bed. "Where are we going?"

"I did some asking and Alex is working down in the ER. I figured what better way for you to talk to her than pay her a little visit."

Jess slipped into the chair with Terra's help. As she tucked her robe around herself, she again had to laugh. "This is insane."

Terra clapped her on the shoulder. "You bet. That's why I know it will work."

* * *

Maria leaned into the exam room as Alex finished with a young boy who had broken his arm jumping off the roof with a parachute made out of a tablecloth. "Hey Doc, something out here you've got to see."

"Okay, be there in a second." Alex turned back to the young boy, who was doing much better than his harried parents. "So, what have we learned here?"

With a sheepish grin, the boy lowered his eyes. "To not jump off the roof."

"That's right. You're not a bird." Alex turned to his parents. "He'll be just fine after we get a cast on him. Six weeks and he'll be good as new." She offered them a warm smile although she didn't feel it herself. She had been walking around in a hollow fog.

Alex finished up and stepped into the hall. Her chest seized as she took in the sight—Jess in a wheelchair being pushed by Terra. And wearing scrubs. "What…" She called out, her voice echoing before she stopped. She took five quick steps and this time lowered her voice to barely above a whisper. "What the hell are you two doing? Jess, you shouldn't be gallivanting around the hospital. What if something happened and you tore out your drain?" She turned to Terra. "And you…you shouldn't be letting her…her…what the hell?"

"What?" Terra smiled at Alex looking completely unfazed.

Alex shook her head. "I can't believe you two. What are you doing down here?"

Terra answered first. "I'm just going over there." She pointed to the nurses' station. "You two talk."

Alex watched Terra walk away. "What are you doing here? You shouldn't be down here."

Jess cleared her throat. "I had to say I'm sorry. I'm sorry for being such a bitch. I know you were only trying to be kind. And

how did I treat you? Not for shit. You didn't deserve that. I need you. I need you in my life. And yes, I even need you to hold my hand sometimes. Can you ever forgive me?"

Alex simply stared. Who was this woman sitting in front of her? Surely it couldn't be the Jess she knew, the Jess who was so adamantly against any assistance from anyone. She slowly smiled. "On one condition."

Jess winced as she lifted her head to meet Alex's eyes. "And what might that be?"

Alex couldn't hold it back any longer. "That when you get out of here, you owe me a race. What do you say to that?"

Jess smiled and shook her head. "I don't know. Do you think you can keep up with me?"

"Oh yeah, Wheels. I'll be right at your side at all costs. Forever."

"And I'll be right there with you, Legs. At all costs."

Terra called out, her voice echoing. "Tell her you love her."

Alex stared at Jess as her face turned red. She raised her eyebrow.

Jess swallowed. "I love you, Legs."

Alex dropped to her knee and wrapped her arms around Jess. "I love you too, Wheels."

And as they kissed, clapping rang throughout the ER.